i

SCP CASE FILES

LEGENDS & MYTHS

ISSUED BY THE O5 COUNCIL

CONTENTS

SCP-3121

Item #: SCP-3121

Object Class: Safe

Location in Fontainebleau, France, where SCP-3121 was recovered

Special Containment Procedures: SCP-3121 is contained in Shelf C, Cage 8 of the Safe Miniature Biological (SaMBio) containment corridor at Site 66. Provisional diet is one tablespoon of nutrient-supplemented fruit mix[1], twice daily. One fresh, living mealworm larva is also to be offered as food once a week, dependent on good behavior.

Allowing SCP-3121 to craft tools and structures reduces outward signs of distress. Dependent on good behavior, raw materials such as straw, small sticks, and leaves may be introduced into SCP-3121's cage. SCP-3121's stick hut, which it has constructed using enrichment materials, is not to be replaced when cleaning.

Description: SCP-3121 is a sapient humanoid measuring 9.8 cm in height. In addition to its small stature, the entity displays other deviations from standard human morphology. SCP-3121's skin is sea green in tone, and covered in wart-like nodules. It also possesses exaggerated facial features, including a heavy brow, prominent cheekbones, and markedly pointed ears, nose and chin. Its overall appearance is reminiscent of an imp or hobgoblin in European folklore.

Aside from its appearance, SCP-3121 is not known to exhibit any other anomalous traits at present[2]. Its biological functions and requirements appear to be as expected of a similarly sized non-anomalous mammal. SCP-3121 displays both primary and secondary masculine sexual characteristics.

SCP-3121 speaks in a dialect similar to Middle High German, a form of the German language spoken between the 11th and 14th centuries. Dr Lena Reiterer, a Foundation linguist with some fluency in a later form of the language, Early New High German, is able to hold conversations with the entity. SCP-3121 is currently uncooperative in interviews, displaying behavioral signs of distress and continually asking for the whereabouts of its "wife".

SCP-3121 was originally found in the Forest of Fontainebleau in northern France on 2005-10-13, inhabiting a crudely constructed hut made from sticks. Materials found within suggest inhabitation for two entities; it is believed that the "wife" mentioned by SCP-3121 was near the site at the time of initial retrieval, but evaded capture without being seen by containment personnel.

Addenda:

DATE   2005-10-15 11:29 UTC

INTERVIEWER   Dr Lena Reiterer

SUPERVISED BY Senior Researcher Jacob Currie (Sentient Containment Specialist)

Dialogue translated from archaic High German unless noted otherwise.

DR REITERER: Hello, SCP-3121.

[SCP-3121 runs to the corner of the cage and cowers.]

DR REITERER: How is it going? Is everything good with you?

SCP-3121: What do you want from me? I— I beg you, let me leave this place. I want to leave.

DR REITERER: I appreciate that. You likely find this place very strange.

[No dialogue for 11 seconds.]

DR REITERER: Do you understand me?

[No dialogue for 5 seconds.]

SCP-3121: Yes.

DR REITERER: I'm glad to hear that. I don't want to hurt you. I just want to ask you some questions about yourself. May I?

[SCP-3121 is silent.]

DR REITERER: Can you—

SR CURRIE: *[in English]* Tell the anomaly that it risks being punished if it doesn't cooperate.

DR REITERER: *[in English]* I— I don't think that's necessary yet. I mean, we're only getting started.

SR CURRIE: *[in English]* We should exploit this fear response. It works on sapients, especially early in containment. Trust me on this.

DR REITERER: *[to SCP-3121]* SCP-3121, your life here will be better if you answer my questions. Where do you come from?

[SCP-3121 is silent.]

DR REITERER: How old are you? Do you know?

[SCP-3121 is silent.]

DR REITERER: Are there other people like you? That is to say, other creatures who look like you?

[SCP-3121 makes a groaning noise.]

SCP-3121: I beg you, let me go. My wife is surely worried about me. I want— I want to return to my wife. She is surely looking for me. I want to see my wife. Let me leave. I want to see my wife.

SR CURRIE: *[in English]* What did the anomaly say?

DR REITERER: *[in English]* It's talking about his— about its wife. The anomaly is saying that it wants to go back to its wife, that the wife will be looking for it.

SR CURRIE: *[in English]* Good, a point of vulnerability. We can exploit that if necessary. Keep going.

DR REITERER: *[to SCP-3121]* Where do you think your wife is? We can bring her to you.

SCP-3121: I won't tell you. You can't catch her, she is too *swinde*[3]. She is cleverer than me, she won't be caught like I was. Just let me go to her. Let me leave this place and go to her.

DR REITERER: *[in English]* I asked it where we could find the wife. It said that it wouldn't tell us, and that we can't catch her because she's too clever and - fierce, I think was the word.

SR CURRIE: *[in English]* Right, this is getting nowhere. The anomaly clearly is not yet acclimatized to containment. I'm terminating this interview now at

— time, thirty-two minutes past eleven. Reasons given: uncooperative subject, low priority due to minimal risk.

DR REITERER: *[in English]* Could I have a little more time to—

[AUDIO ENDS]

Supervisor comments: I have now read the translated log. The risk of negative consequences for non-compliance was not made as clearly as it could have been. This should be corrected in the next interview.

We need to locate this "wife".

— Senior Researcher Jacob Currie

SCP-3121 IS A DEVELOPING PHENOMENON. THE BELOW DOCUMENTATION IS PROVISIONAL AND SUBJECT TO CHANGE.

Item #: SCP-3121

Object Class: Keter

Special Containment Procedures: SCP-3121-A (previously SCP-3121) is to be contained according to previous procedures. *Change pending.*

Locating and containing SCP-3121-B is a high priority. Foundation data crawlers are to monitor mentions of possible SCP-3121-B activity in all surveillance vectors, including internet traffic, civilian phone messages, security camera feeds, and emergency service radio. If an SCP-3121-B sighting is suspected, the nearest available Mobile Task Force is to be immediately deployed to SCP-3121-B's last known location. All surviving witnesses of SCP-3121-B activity are to be located and amnesticised at the earliest opportunity.

Description: SCP-3121-A (previously SCP-3121) is a sapient humanoid measuring 9.8 cm in height, similar in appearance to imps or hobgoblins of European folklore. SCP-3121-A has masculine primary and secondary sexual characteristics, and is capable of speech in a dialect similar to Middle High German. The Foundation currently holds SCP-3121-A in containment.

SCP-3121-B is a sapient humanoid similar to SCP-3121-A. SCP-3121-B is uncontained, hostile, and dangerous. According to video evidence, SCP-3121-B has the anomalous ability of travelling long distances instantaneously by entering the cranial cavities of human beings.

It is believed that SCP-3121-B is the "wife" character previously mentioned by SCP-3121-A.

Addenda:

LOCATION Zagreb, Croatia

DATE   2005-10-23 09:13 (07:13 UTC)

SOURCE   Security camera footage

NOTE: NO AUDIO.

Still from 09:13:50

09:13:43 - 09:13:52 Pedestrians walk on the street. Three cars drive past on the adjacent road. No unusual activity present.

09:13:53 - 09:13:57 In the bottom-right of the frame, a bald man facing away from the camera suddenly stops walking, clutching the back of his head with his left hand.

09:13:59 - 09:14:06 The man - later identified as Tamás Novák, 54 years old - loses balance, bracing himself against the wall with his arm.

09:14:07 - 09:14:18 The bald man falls against the wall to a crouched sitting position, clutching his head with both hands. A middle-aged woman in a green shawl carrying a shopping bag jogs into view from the bottom of the frame.

6

She stops next to the man and leans towards him, apparently concerned for his well-being.

09:14:19 - 09:14:31 A young man in a black coat walks over to observe the situation and exchanges some brief words with the woman in the green shawl; he then begins to make a call on his mobile phone. The bald man crouched against the wall begins to shake violently. Witnesses report him moaning loudly at this point.

09:14:32 - 09:14:40 The bald man, still facing away from the camera, stops shaking and falls still. Three seconds later, the woman in the green shawl stands up abruptly, falling onto her back. The view shows the apparent reason for this: the back of the bald man's scalp has been suddenly split open by a large gash. Rhythmic movement of a small light-coloured object can be observed within the wound, which coincides with the bald man's head jerking slightly, as if his head is being opened from the inside.

09:14:34 - 09:14:39 Three more persons approach the scene from various positions. The wound is increasing in size and bleeding profusely; all bystanders appear to be reacting with panic.

09:14:40 - 09:14:45 The wound in the man's head bulges. A small figure about 10 cm in height bursts from the gash and leaps to the ground. Chaos ensues. All bystanders jump and run to move away from the small entity - except for the middle-aged woman in the green shawl, who is still lying on her back after having fallen.

09:14:46 - 09:14:56 Two male bystanders flee the scene. The small figure looks around, pointing at several individuals. Witnesses report it repeating a phrase in an unknown language as it does so. The figure then clambers up onto the face of the middle-aged woman lying on the floor.

09:14:57 - 09:15:10 Blood quickly pools on the pavement below the woman as she clutches at her temples and throat. Autopsy examination indicates that the small figure used a slashing implement to sever several arteries in the woman's neck and face while climbing onto her head. The small figure stoops down over the woman's face; it is not clear from the footage, but witnesses report the small figure at this point slicing at the woman's left eye.

09:15:11 - 09:15:19 The woman paws weakly at her throat, which is still gushing blood. Remaining bystanders shout and gesture in distress, but none step forward to intervene. The small figure stops slicing and disappears into the woman's face, apparently entering through the left eye socket.

09:15:20 - 09:15:25 The woman's head jerks slightly, and is then still. Dark fumes rise out of her head.

09:15:26 - 09:15:30 A can rolls out of the dead woman's shopping bag and onto the road. It is run over by a car. Red liquid sprays onto the asphalt.

LOCATION Osaka, Japan

DATE   2005-10-23 16:15 (07:15 UTC)

SOURCE   Security camera footage

NOTE: WHEN TIME ZONES ARE TAKEN INTO ACCOUNT, THE FOLLOWING FOOTAGE BEGINS IMMEDIATELY AFTER THE END OF VIDEO 1. NO AUDIO.

Still from 16:15:32

16:15:30 - 16:15:38 A group of eight adolescents are standing in a circle.

16:15:39 - 16:15:45 One member of the group drops to the floor, grabbing the back of their head with both hands.

[ADDITIONAL LOGS REMOVED]

Situation Report, 24/10/2005, SR Jacob Currie

SCP-3121-A told us in interview that its "wife" would be looking for it. It seems that the anomaly was correct to state this.

The activities of this wife, SCP-3121-B, are described as follows. It cuts into the heads of humans, through the eyes most often, and penetrates a thin segment of skull. Witnesses report that the anomaly uses a large metal nail to do this. It enters the brain and performs an unknown action. Then, SCP-3121-B and a perfect sphere of cerebral tissue disappear, leaving a hot, cauterized hole in the human's brain.

SCP-3121-B reappears in the brain of another human somewhere else on the planet and exits by cutting through the back of that person's head. It can then repeat the above process on a different individual. The travel between brains is instantaneous. No distance limit or pattern in the travel of SCP-3121-B has been observed. Analysis indicates that the human SCP-3121-B manifests in is chosen randomly.

We have audio samples of SCP-3121-B speaking to witnesses. Ms Reiterer tells me that the anomaly speaks the same language as SCP-3121-A, and the speech translates to questions about the location of SCP-3121-B's "husband". Curse words are also present.

Containing SCP-3121-B is of high importance. SCP-3121-B activity is frequent and unpredictable. The activity often occurs in public places. Only two of the forty-eight civilians who have been host to SCP-3121-B's ability have survived. Both suffer from extreme and permanent brain damage due to the large volume of missing tissue.

Concealing the many deaths and amnesticising witnesses is a drain on resources. SCP-3121-B activity occurring on live broadcast or to a high-profile individual would be major emergency. The current situation represents a severe information breach.

SCP-3121-A has not been compliant in providing information on SCP-3121-B and its anomalous travel ability. To increase the likelihood of obtaining this information, I have deprived the anomaly of all privileges and instituted more stringent interrogation techniques.

- Acting Head of SCP-3121 Containment, SR Jacob Currie

Locations of individuals known to have hosted SCP-3121-B's travel ability prior to containment

Special Containment Procedures: SCP-3121-A and SCP-3121-B are to be contained separately. Each is to be contained in airlocked chambers suitable for high-risk intelligent anomalies. Human contact is to be avoided when possible, in order to minimize the risk of the entities utilizing their anomalous travel ability.

Additional care is to be taken with SCP-3121-B, which is hostile and aggressive. SCP-3121-B should be physically restrained at all times, with additional restraints added during interviews or other necessary close interactions.

Description: SCP-3121-A and -B are small, sapient humanoids measuring approximately 10 cm in height, similar in appearance to imps or hobgoblins in European folklore. According to sexual characteristics, SCP-3121-A is of male sex, and SCP-3121-B female. Both entities are capable of speech in a dialect similar to Middle High German.

SCP-3121-B has demonstrated an anomalous ability to travel instantly between the brains of human beings. It is unknown whether SCP-3121-A also possesses this ability.

SCP-3121-A was originally acquired alone at a location in the Forest of Fontainebleau, France, on 2005-10-13. It is presumed that SCP-3121-B observed the containment of SCP-3121-A without being seen by containment personnel. One week later, on 2005-10-21, SCP-3121-B began utilizing its anomalous travel ability in an apparent search for SCP-3121-A, which it describes as its "husband". 141 individuals across 48 countries are known to have been affected by SCP-3121-B's travel activity, of which 135 subsequently died due to traumatic brain injury.

SCP-3121-B was contained in rural Bangladesh, having manifesting in the head of a woman wearing a motorcycle helmet and being unable to break through the headgear. The female victim was then admitted to a local hospital as an apparent stroke victim, where medical staff noticed scraping sounds and

10

muffled shouts emanating from her helmet. Mobile Task Force Xi-8 ("Spearhunters") were able to capture the entity at the site.

Addenda:

DATE   2005-10-31 15:05 UTC

INTERVIEWER   Dr Lena Reiterer

SUPERVISED BY Senior Researcher Jacob Currie (Head of Containment, SCP-3121)

Dialogue translated from archaic High German unless noted otherwise.

NOTE: For the duration of this interview, SCP-3121-B had been restrained to a chair capable of delivering electric shocks to the occupant.

SCP-3121-B: *[Continued from previous unrecorded dialogue]* —devil, you are unspeakable deformities, both of you. Cowardly lice, worms, pathetic worms! I curse your entire race to the endless torment of eighteen hells. You blood-shamed plague, hateful savages, the disgrace of the Earth's—

[SR CURRIE administers an electric shock to silence SCP-3121-B.]

DR REITERER: SCP-3121-B, you have to talk to us. I want to talk to you without you being hurt. It would be better for everyone.

[SCP-3121-B breathes heavily and wipes its mouth with its hand.]

SCP-3121-B: I know that you will kill me in this place. I do not fear death, you murderers.

DR REITERER: You likely will not believe me, but I swear that we do not want you to die. We do not want that.

SCP-3121-B: Do you think me a fool? How could I ever trust any of your kind? Your kind, who carried out such slaughter upon my people! Centuries of slaughter! As if we were crawling vermin of the mud! You disgusting rot. Have you not killed enough of us? We are nearly snuffed out, perished. My husband and I have not seen another of our kind for two hundred years. Are we the last ones left? Is this what you're doing? *[Laughter.]* Are you ending us once and for all? Bastard devils! Evil from the dark pits of the fetid pools in—

DR REITERER: *[in English, to SR CURRIE]* Don't give another shock. This is useful.

DR REITERER: *[to SCP-3121-B]* SCP-3121-B, when you were travelling through people's heads, what was your aim?

SCP-3121-B: I don't understand your vulgar words. What are you saying?

DR REITERER: I'm sorry. What were you seeking when you went inside heads and appeared in a different place?

SCP-3121-B: I was seeking my husband! You surely have him here. I can sense his presence[?][4]. I know it.

DR REITERER: Why do you want to see him?

SCP-3121-B: Why? How can you not understand? You truly are monsters. I have lived with and loved that man these past eight hundred years. We have poured our hearts into each other for ten of your lifetimes – ten. Fleeting, candle-flicker mayflies as you are, you cannot understand the depth of love that we have built together. My living is worthless without him. There is nothing I would not—

[SR CURRIE administers an electric shock to silence SCP-3121-B.]

DR REITERER: *[in English, to SR CURRIE]* No! What are you doing?

SCP-3121-B: Bastards! You dung, filthy— *[screeching, presumed cursing, too high a pitch to be deciphered]*

SR CURRIE: *[in English]* I read anger from the anomaly's behaviour.

DR REITERER: *[in English]* It was intensity, not anger. She was providing information – useful information.

SCP-3121-B: *[continued screeching]*

SR CURRIE: *[in English]* The anomaly was providing information. You do not use personal pronouns when referring to objects in containment. That is basic protocol.

SCP-3121-B: *[continued screeching]*

SR CURRIE: *[in English]* But yes, this course of events is… is disappointing. I will have to rethink the approach. I don't believe SCP-3121-B will be willing to talk to us in this session. We will have to try again a different time.

[No dialogue for 3 seconds.]

DR REITERER: Clearly.

[AUDIO ENDS]

Supervisor comments: The interview was unsuccessful. SCP-3121-A and SCP-3121-B are not providing sufficient information.

It is important to discover more about SCP-3121-B's unique method of instantaneous travel. I am planning an interrogation procedure based on the emotional responses observed in interviews. It is designed to apply a maximally intense acute emotional stressor on SCP-3121-B. I expect it to reduce SCP-3121-B's defiance and sense of superiority. This will make useful answers more likely.

— Senior Researcher Jacob Currie, Head of SCP-3121 Containment

Senior Researcher Currie conducted a psychological stress exercise on both SCP-3121-A and -B today at 17:00. Senior Researcher Currie placed SCP-3121-A into the shock chair used in the interview logged above. SCP-3121-B was also restrained in the same room, and forced to watch as Senior Researcher Currie applied increasingly strong electric shocks to SCP-3121-A. Notably, this was the first time since their containment that SCP-3121-A and SCP-3121-B had seen each other.

Twenty-five minutes into the exercise, SCP-3121-B broke free of its restraints and incapacitated Senior Researcher Currie before subjecting him to [REDACTED]. After this, SCP-3121-B used Senior Researcher Currie's corpse to activate its travel ability, and disappeared with SCP-3121-A. As of this incident, SCP-3121-A and SCP-3121-B are now considered to be uncontained, and their whereabouts unknown.

Dr Lena Reiterer, previously translator in SCP-3121 interviews, has been promoted to Head of Containment for SCP-3121 in the light of Senior Researcher Currie's death.

Aerial photograph with SCP-3121's containment site outlined

Object Class: Keter (see Addendum: SCP-3121 Object Class Status)

Special Containment Procedures: SCP-3121-A and -B are to be contained on-site at their current location in the forests of Småland, Sweden. An exclusion zone 400 m x 400 m centered around SCP-3121's main habitation structure is to be maintained, patrolled by two guards and surrounded by antimemetic fencing to dissuade passersby from entering.

Containment activities are to be carried out so that Foundation personnel are not seen by SCP-3121-A and -B, as experience to date suggests that they remain non-hostile as long as they do not witness human beings.

Description: SCP-3121-A and -B are small, sapient humanoids measuring approximately 10 cm in height. The entities resemble imps or hobgoblins from European folklore. According to morphological sexual characteristics, SCP-3121-A is male, and SCP-3121-B female; the entities describe each other as "husband" and "wife", and display a strong emotional attachment.

The entities have human-level intelligence, speaking a dialect similar to Middle High German. They display high proficiency in tool-making and wilderness survival, which they use to practice a hunter-gatherer lifestyle. Their diet consists mainly of berries, tubers, and insects.

Previous interviews with SCP-3121-B suggest that the entities are at least 800 years old. The same interviews suggest that SCP-3121-A and -B are one of the few – possibly only – surviving members of what was once a more numerous population of similar beings.

SCP-3121-A and -B were previously contained at Site-66, before an incident in which a Foundation employee, Senior Researcher Currie, [REDACTED][5].

Abandoned hunting shack used by SCP-3121 as their main habitation structure

Two years later, on 2007-08-03, the SCP-3121 entities were discovered at their present location in Småland, Sweden, and current containment procedures were implemented.

No hostile activity has been displayed by either SCP-3121 entity since their escape together from initial containment. All observations of SCP-3121 at their current site have shown them engaging in domestic activities, creating handicrafts, and taking walks around the containment site, usually while holding hands.

Addenda:

2017-11-05: Senior Researcher Lena Reiterer, Head of SCP-3121 Containment, has applied for SCP-3121 to be downgraded from Keter to Euclid after 12 years of docile behavior. The application has passed the first round of review.

Footnotes

1. Note to containment technicians: same as the mix given to SCP-1192 housed on the shelf above.

2. Note: SCP-3121 was only recently brought into containment, so the full extent of its properties is yet to be determined through testing.

3. Can be translated variously as *strong*, *angry* or *quick*.

4. Literally: *I feel his air*.

5. For further information, see *Ketergrams 2005*. In a post-incident review, Senior Researcher Currie's conduct during interrogations of SCP-3121 was found to be in breach of the Foundation's ethical guidelines for intelligent anomaly containment.

SCP-082

Item #: SCP-082

Object Class: Euclid

Special Containment Procedures: Enlarged living quarters located at Armed Bio-Containment Area-14 have been appropriated for the suppression and appeasement of SCP-082. While standard weapons have little effect in policing SCP-082, cooperation is easily attained through a charade; subject is currently under the impression that it has been made the King of France and that its containment area is actually a grand palace designed for its protection. All interacting personnel are to be made aware of this charade and are ordered to follow the ruse. Housekeeping personnel are to be Class D personnel only.

Guards tasked with the containment of SCP-082 are to be given Level-2 clearance, but are instructed to refrain from interacting directly with SCP-082.

Description: SCP-082 is genetically human; however, through some process (either chemical, hormonal, cancerous, or supernatural), SCP-082 has grown to giant proportions. Approximately 2.4 meters tall (around 8 ft) and weighing over 310 kg (about 700 lb), SCP-082's physical characteristics are grossly disproportional. It has a slightly pointed balding head, a large rounded chin and jaw, a bulbous nose, and dark sunken eyes. Subject is both overweight and possesses a great amount of muscle mass. Forearms are muscular and dangerous, with a circumference of about 71 cm (about 28 in). The breadth of the subject's fist is nearly 30 cm along the knuckles (almost 12 in). Though feet are large, they are small in proportion to subject's body (men's size 14 US). Subject's skin is tanned dark and overall physical appearance is compounded by numerous scars (the results of years of attempts at suppression and containment). Most X-rays have been difficult to interpret because of the high density of its muscle tissue, but scans have revealed countless bullets and even several knife and sword blades lodged in SCP-082's flesh.

SCP-082 refers to itself as Fernand and speaks fluent French and heavily accented English. When it speaks, it does so through enormous, clenched teeth. SCP-082 only parts teeth to eat food and to sing. Subject will sing songs of its own pleasing, ranging from forgotten Victorian Era bar songs to modern classical, typically while cooking and eating. SCP-082 does not comb the hair on the sides of its head, but does cut it, and shaves with a large butcher knife originally provided for food preparation. It should be noted that even facial hair is exaggerated, a single strand being as thick as a millimeter (similar in thickness and appearance to graphite of a mechanical pencil). Occasionally, SCP-082 will clench its teeth so hard that the gums bleed, but it is not known why. This is considered normal.

The demeanor of SCP-082 is very amicable and carefree. SCP-082 has accrued a wide wardrobe over its time of incarceration, and it enjoys dressing up in many different fashions, including formal wear, military uniform, as a clown, and in women's clothing. New pieces should be made available upon request. Subject often attempts to joke and is usually polite to personnel, often inviting them to dinner. However, visiting personnel should be aware that at any moment, SCP-082 is capable of attacking and voraciously eating others. Subject will often apologize for its lack of manners for interrupting someone's conversation by devouring their head while making a mess of his quarters. SCP-082's jaw is strong enough to crack bone, and it seems to enjoy skulls. Attacks are seemingly at random with no motivation—whether or not subject has recently eaten has no effect on this cannibalistic hunger.

SCP-082 is incapable of differentiating fact from fiction when he reads it or watches television/films. On several occasions, SCP-082 has expressed a great desire to meet his favorite person, Hannibal Lecter, and subject will believe that all television programming is some form of reality television. Though subject has shown heightened intelligence in the form of memory and puzzle-solving, the concepts of parody, satire, and fiction are beyond its understanding. SCP-082 apparently understands the concept of lying, has shown to know when others are blatantly lying, and generally tells obvious falsehoods when asked about its past. According to SCP-082, he is:

- A vampire

- A homunculus

- Big Bird

- André the Giant

- Napoleon

- Obelix (sidekick of Asterix)

- Dr. Bright

- The Hulk

- Alexander The Great

- Captain Hook

- Sherlock Holmes

- Dr. Frankenstein

- Frankenstein's Monster

When questioned about these lies he gives the excuse, "But I only lie when it's through my teeth!"

SCP-140

Item #: SCP-140

Object Class: Keter

A reproduction of SCP-140

Special Containment Procedures: SCP-140 must never be brought closer than 15 m to any source of standard ink, human blood, or other fluids suitable for writing. Any contamination by blood or ink must be reported immediately. Any remaining copies of SCP-140 created during the initial printing must be found and destroyed as soon as possible. Only SCP-140 is to be preserved, for purposes of study, early warning, and cataloguing and recording possible SCPs derived from its subject matter.

SCP-140 is contained at Site-76 in a sealed vault containing a single desk. At this time no research is to be carried out upon the original SCP-140; researchers are to read from prepared copies not bearing the signature of its author which lack its properties. In the event of approved research, SCP-140 may not be removed from the vault, and readers may not be in contact with it for longer than 9 hours. Access requires written approval from the head researcher for the explicit purposes of testing. An armed guard stationed outside the vault will meet any attempted theft with deadly force.

Should any personnel begin displaying obsession with SCP-140 or signs of possible memetic contamination, they are to be issued a Class A Amnestic, false memories implanted as necessary, and transferred to another project. Transferred personnel must be monitored for signs of relapse.

Description: SCP-140 is a modern hardcopy book with an unremarkable black binding and an unknown number of white pages. The book jacket is missing, but the title, "A Chronicle of the Daevas", is clearly legible. The inside cover is signed by the author, whose name is indecipherable. The text is copyrighted 19█. Careful examination reveals there are far more pages between the bindings than could be contained within them.

Readers admit to feelings of paranoia, unease, and occasional nausea while reading SCP-140, although this may be related to the subject material. Nonetheless, readers almost universally describe SCP-140 as fascinating and express continued interest, despite its frequently unsettling content. One in fifteen readers describe SCP-140 as having a faint odor of dried blood.

SCP-140 is a detailed account of an ancient civilization originating in what is now south-central Siberia, identified as the Daevites. Although like all cultures the Daevites evolved and changed over time, they appear to have exhibited unusual continuity. Universal fixtures of the Daevite culture in all periods included militarism, conquest, ancestor worship, urban centers ruling over large slave populations, gruesome human sacrifice, and the practice of apparently efficacious thaumaturgic rituals. A variety of relics and creatures produced by the Daevite culture would be abnormal or dangerous enough, if the account is to be believed, to qualify for containment in their own right.

If SCP-140 comes into contact with any fluid suitable for writing, including human blood, the account of the Daevite civilization's history expands. Human blood appears the most "potent" of possible writing substances, but in any case the amount of new material does not correspond proportionately to the fluids introduced. Although these new segments sometimes include new descriptions of rituals or cultural traits or illustrations of previously covered material, they more frequently include new, more recent accounts of information chronicling the continued history of the Daevite civilization or descriptions of new individuals and artifacts. Formerly decisive defeats become setbacks; new persons and events are inserted. Foundation archaeologists have discovered corresponding new artifacts and traces of the Daevite civilization in applicable locations and strata, in some cases found in dig sites that had already been thoroughly explored.

Although at times the Daevites were a collection of city-states, they appear to have consistently returned to imperialism under a theocratic aristocracy (the "daeva"), practitioners of cannibalism and thaumaturgy. Although initially Foundation researchers believed the daeva to have been a hereditary class recycling the names of noteworthy individuals, evidence and the events of █-██-20██ now suggest that the daeva possessed preternatural longevity as a result of [REDACTED]. Several researchers, notably Professor ████████, have concluded the daeva were so divergent from modern humans as to be a separate subspecies, a conclusion supported by graphic representations within SCP-140 and [DATA EXPUNGED].

SCP-140 is remarkably detailed by the standards of a primary source, seeming closer to a biography than a historic text. It includes lurid descriptions of sacrificial rites, battlefield descriptions, daily life, and the life stories of various noteworthy individuals including quotes and dates of birth. Over ██ distinct individuals have been identified including the individual presently termed SCP-140-A, of which only ██ are accounted for by recorded deaths.

Foundation archaeologists have discovered several sites containing ruins consistent with the supposed Daevite culture in various locations across Siberia, northern Iran, and Mongolia. Artifacts and traces of inter-cultural conflict and contact have been discovered as far west as the Carpathian Mountains and as far east as northern Pakistan and China. These include SCP-[REDACTED].

Addendum 140a:
SCP-140 was originally found in the office of deceased historian ██████ ██████. The previous owner was discovered in his office at █████ University, having expired from self-inflicted lacerations on both wrists. There were no traces of ██████'s blood in the office. ██████'s colleagues claimed during interviews they discovered a note in faded ink in ██████'s handwriting next to SCP-140. All witnesses were administered Class A Amnesiacs and false memories implanted.

██████'s note read:

I have to know. I'm sorry.

All texts within 15 m except several books relating to the history of the region were blank; the remaining books now included accounts of supposed interaction between the Daevite civilization and the subject cultures or applicable discussions of Daevite history and culture. These texts were confiscated. All printed forms and media were blank. All pens, printers, and ink cartridges were empty.

Addendum 140b:
Although SCP-140 was published during the 20th century, the tone of the book suggests it is a recounting of events, individuals, and practices experienced firsthand by SCP-140's unknown author. Foundation investigators have tracked SCP-140's publication to the [DATA EXPUNGED] printing house in a batch of ██ copies self-published by a wealthy individual hereby termed SCP-140-A. SCP-140-A's signature on the contract matches the strange signature inside SCP-140.

More than 4█ of the copies produced in this batch were apparently leeched of all ink by the █ remaining copies. To date, Foundation agents have recovered and destroyed ██ of the remainder, but between █ and ██ remain at large. Two expansion events have been reported during periods when SCP-140 had never been exposed to fluids of any sort or removed from its vault.

An investigation and manhunt for the author of SCP-140 is ongoing. In the event of contact, agents are advised [DATA REDACTED].

Addendum 140c:
Through study of SCP-140 and other contained objects related to the Daevite civilization, Foundation researchers have concluded that, transposed to the

modern era, the resurgence of a hostile Daevite civilization in history more recent than 1██ CE would constitute a grave and even possibly retroactive threat to the Foundation and modern civilization as we know it. Even best-case projections of Daevite resurgence in the modern day suggest a CK-class restructuring of modern society and a worldwide conflict with a projected death toll of at least [REDACTED] and an end to the Foundation's secrecy.

Addendum 140d:

██████ ██████'s journal, found on his home PC in [DATA EXPUNGED], indicates that upon his initial reading of SCP-140, it ended with the almost utter destruction of the Daevite civilization and the genocide of all known daeva in 2██ BCE by the forces of Chinese general Qin Kai. As a result of subsequent containment breaches, including those detailed in the journal, copious quantities of new material have been added, describing survivors regrouping and migrating to another region of central Siberia, rebuilding their empire steadily, and continuing to advance culturally and technologically. At present, the empire is described as having finally been crushed by Genghis Khan during the early period of his conquests, although the fates of many important persons and several cities remain ambiguous. Foundation archaeologists will be dispatched to [EXPUNGED] for investigation and research.

Addendum 140e:

After the incident on █-█-20██ at [DATA EXPUNGED] dig site resulting in over ██ casualties, all Foundation archaeologists excavating sites of suspected Daevite artifacts or ruins are to be accompanied by a fully armed security team. SCP-140-1 has been neutralized. SCP-140-2 remains at large. All other anomalous contacts and artifacts were destroyed when the dig site was struck by a cruise missile. Agent ██████ received a commendation and was treated for post-traumatic stress disorder. Dr. ████ received a posthumous commendation for courage.

An investigation into the possible involvement of SCP-140-A or their agents in the events of █-█-20██ is ongoing.

SCP-1726

Item #: SCP-1726

Object Class: Euclid

Special Containment Procedures: The path leading to SCP-1726 is to be blocked by a guard post operated by the Foundation Chinese Branch under the banner of the People's Liberation Army. No further security is necessary to prevent outside interference.

SCP-1726 itself is not to be entered without at least one instance of SCP-1726-1 accompanying researchers. Personnel are not to remain within SCP-1726 for periods longer than four hours. Materials found within SCP-1726 are not to be removed from SCP-1726.

Contact with SCP-1726-1 specimens is to be carried out according to Document 1726-CO.

All documents copied within SCP-1726 are to be stored in Research Archive 18.

Description: SCP-1726 is a one-story structure located in [REDACTED] Province, China. No anomalies are present in the materials used to build SCP-1726, and the original construction is estimated to date from around 1200 CE.

The interior of SCP-1726 is a stable spatial anomaly, measuring approximately fourteen square kilometers in area. This space consists of a library, surrounding a small garden and fountain. The contents of this library consist primarily of philosophical, theological, and historical texts, accompanied by artifacts from civilizations in east and central Asia, many of which originate from cultures unknown to general anthropology. The oldest artifacts contained within SCP-1726 are a collection of Yeren tablets dated to approximately 30000 BCE. Other notable civilizations featured are the Shambhalan dynasties, the Lemurian river peoples, the dynasties of Mu, and the Daevic Empire.

A stone pillar rises out of the central garden of SCP-1726, ascending through a hole in the roof to an unknown height and climbable by means of a wooden walkway spiraling around the edge of the structure. This pillar exists within the spatial anomaly of SCP-1726, and so is not able to be seen from the outside. The exact height is unknown: the highest point reached by Foundation agents is 12.8 km.

SCP-1726-1 is a group of fifty-four known humanoid constructs, composed of porcelain. Constructs are hollow, capable of full articulation, and will generally appear to be stylized representations of scholarly cultural archetypes. SCP-1726-1 specimens are sapient, and are fluent in various dialects of modern and ancient Chinese languages, and other obscure or extinct dialects. SCP-1726-1-03, SCP-1726-1-20, and SCP-1726-1-44 are fluent in English. SCP-1726-1 behavior generally consists of studying the contents of SCP-1726, and in guiding visitors through SCP-1726.

When an individual remains outside SCP-1726 for an extended period of time (one to six hours), a specimen of SCP-1726-1 will emerge from the structure and offer to lead the individual in a tour of the library. Upon returning to the entryway, the SCP-1726-1 instance will speak the following phrase in classical Chinese: "I have wandered a great distance, and I have learned ten thousand things." Unaccompanied entry into SCP-1726, even after using the appropriate verbal cue, will result in immediate expulsion from the structure by an unseen force. Extended time spent within SCP-1726 (over four hours) will result in disorientation, memory loss, and nausea due to the spatial compression effects. Climbing the central pillar will not generate this effect.

Addendum-01: Notable excerpts from texts include:

"And as I looked back, I saw that my home was lost to the Beast's stirring. The boat was shaken by the waves, as I watched the last fires on the hills of Mu die out. Despair clutches at my heart, for so much had been lost in our foolishness."

Taken from "The Records of the Destruction of Mu", (c. 25000 BCE), a collection of short tales from one Kai-Zuun-Loo, a survivor of the destruction of the continent.

"The Daevas returned in triumph, Ab-Leshal at the front of the column of soldiers and great war-beasts that did stretch to the horizon, bringing with them trophies of bronze from far-off lands and peoples in chains to the work in their slave pits. I watched, and I knew fear."

Taken from Fragment C of "The Traveler's Book" (c. 11000 BCE), records of an unnamed individual observing the Daevic Empire. Event described is the triumphal march of Daeva Hhu Rie in 11039 BCE, as is further described in other records of the Low Daevic period.

"Look here, look there, look behind and look forward. All things are connected, just as the lines of these words are connected, and the cycle turns ever more. Look to those who thought themselves gods: they were cast down by those they have enslaved. Slaves become masters, to be thrown down by their own slaves, and so the cycle goes, forever, until the Earth is blackened and the last stars have died. For the Great Ones have passed, and Mu has passed, and the lands to the South and the West have passed, and even the Empire has passed."

A quote from an unknown work, found in Scroll 8 of "Tya Jhalil", (c. 9000 BCE), a compendium of philosophy written in the aftermath of the collapse of the Daevic Empire.

[Illegible] was here.

Graffiti carved on the fountain in the center garden, date unknown, presumed to be at least 150 years of age. Written in English.

Notable artifacts found within SCP-1726 include:

- 1 non-functioning Eternal Engine dating from the High Daevic period (c. 15000 BCE), with schematics for repair.

- 4 functioning Low Daevic period slave collars (c. 10000 BCE).

- Remains of 2 deceased hexapedal creatures resembling small cetaceans. Origin unknown.

- 6 heavily damaged and inactive fragments of bronze clockwork. Fragments bear carved mantras from the Low Daevic period.

- A sample of tissue from an unknown organism. The tissue contains a high mineral content, and has visible strata within it. Sample is labelled "From the Beast that Destroyed Mu".

- 1 wrought-iron lantern, date unknown. The flame within cannot be extinguished, and the addition of fuel does not generate any change.

- 102 maps of civilizations cataloged within SCP-1726.

Addendum-02: ██/██/20██: An unknown entity was observed by researchers described as a squat humanoid with limbs similar to those of an arachnid. The entity was seen re-arranging books, and upon being seen fled from researchers and ascended the central pillar. General research within SCP-1726 has been halted for the time being.

SCP-2615

Item #: SCP-2615

Object Class: Keter

Special Containment Procedures: Large-scale dissemination of the falsified information to the public that SCP-2615-A are fictional entities is to be continuously carried out. The claims of individuals that SCP-2615 is real are to be discredited. Any photographic, video, textual, or other information confirming the existence of SCP-2615 is either to be discredited or removed from public availability.

A file entitled SCP-2615-J is to be created as a cover for SCP-2615 activity. This file is to be humorous in tone, incorporate modern SCP-2615 stereotypes, and be created using the SCP documentation standardized format. This document is to be filed with a collection of similar documents, all labeled with the suffix "-J" and written as humorous items or anecdotes in the SCP format. This collection of documents may be expanded by personnel, but it is to be made clear that all "-J" files are fictional, and intended only for the purpose of humor. In the event that any personnel without access to SCP-2615 begins to consider the possible existence of SCP-2615, they are to be directed to the SCP-2615-J document.

In the event that a manifestation of SCP-2615 is confirmed, it is to be secured and detained by Mobile Task Forces Eta-12 ("Fe 0C°") and Mu-7 ("Parish Priests") until demanifestation.

Description: SCP-2615 is the collective designation for a species of extra-temporal humanoids (SCP-2615-A) and their civilization and culture (SCP-2615-B). The presence of SCP-2615 in baseline reality is directly related to human acceptance of the concept of SCP-2615 as fact. The more humans which accept the concept of SCP-2615 as fact, the greater the presence of SCP-2615 in our timeline. Similarly, the greater the amount of the population which is aware of SCP-2615's concept without believing it is fact, the less presence SCP-2615 has in our reality.

SCP-2615-A is a species of humanoids. Instances of SCP-2615-A are physiologically very similar to humans, with some notable divergences. The ears of SCP-2615-A taper to a point at the helixes, slightly improving instances' ability to detect low-volume sounds. SCP-2615 instances are also pentachromats[1]. Instances age at a slower rate than humans, with the average natural lifespan being 109 years. Most notably, SCP-2615-A instances possess a small, roughly spherical organ located between the liver and stomach, near the gallbladder. This organ appears connected to the instance's nervous system, and is capable of temporarily causing small disruptions in local reality, granting the instance low-level reality altering abilities.

The psychology of SCP-2615-A also differs from humanity. Instances almost universally possess some form of minor Obsessive Compulsive Disorder. While mostly non-sociopathic, SCP-2615-A instances tend to display highly manipulative tendencies. Finally, SCP-2615-A possess a minimum of two identified emotions with no clear human analogue.

SCP-2615-B designates the civilization and culture of SCP-2615-A instances. From information recorded during SCP-2615 manifestations, Foundation historians have been able to construct a partial history of SCP-2615-B, as it would appear should SCP-2615 ever fully manifest in reality. SCP-2615-B history has been categorized into three main periods, as outlined in Addendum 1.

Addendum 1:

First Era: Unknown - 535 A.D.

The population is primarily composed of tribal groups, located in Northwestern Europe. Agriculture, nomadic, and hunter/forager lifestyles are practiced by different tribes, with some tribes practicing a mixture of lifestyles. Tribes often carry out raids on human groups and other tribes, taking young and juvenile captives and incorporating them into their tribe. Belief systems are mostly shamanistic in nature, and consist of a mixture of polytheistic, monotheistic, and animistic religions. A marked belief of iron as an evil substance exists through several tribes, believed to result from the observation of tetanus infectees. Mutual superstition and suspicion exist between humans and SCP-2615-A. Towards the end of the period, SCP-2615-A tribes begin to unite into larger groups.

Middle Era: 535 A.D. - 1772 A.D.

For approximately a century, the large groups created by the combination of tribes wage constant war against other groups for land, resources, and political power. Near the end of this century, SCP-2615-B stabilizes into 27 distinct nations, the largest and most powerful of which is based in the British Isles and some areas of France, Belgium, the Netherlands, Norway, Germany, and Denmark. In this and 18 of the other nations, SCP-2615-B is composed of self-regulating and self-sustaining groups of extended family, with some intermarriage between family groups, which pay allegiance and tribute to a central monarch.

In 7 of the remaining nations, governing bodies are composed of representative democracies and land is divided into smaller city-states, each regulated by a smaller democratic system composed of the patriarchs and matriarchs of family groups. Each state democracy then would send a representative to the national government. The final nation consisted of a two-party political system, with the two parties referred to as the "Summer Court" and "Winter Court". Each SCP-2615-A instance would decide their party at the age of 15, at which point they were considered an adult. Members of each party were expected to regulate and control other members of their own party. Intermarriage between members of the two parties was forbidden. From late spring to early fall, members of the Summer Court had full control over members of the Winter Court. From late fall to early spring, members of the Winter Court had full control over members of the Summer Court. SCP-2615-A most commonly set up their territories and dwellings in rural areas and areas unpopulated by humans.

Though small territorial disputes occurred over the next millennia, most wars were short, caused little damage, and did not cause any large-scale power shifts. From the fifteenth to seventeenth centuries, SCP-2615-B nations began to create colonies across Europe, Africa, Asia, and the Americas.

During this time period, there is a marked increase in the presence of anomalies in SCP-2615-B. In most cases, low-level anomalies are utilized by SCP-2615-A for entertainment and utility. In other cases, high-level anomalies form the basis for religions.

During this period, there is a slight increase in human/SCP-2615 interactions. Though still rare, SCP-2615 instances will occasionally enter business agreements with humans for an exchange of goods or services. SCP-2615-A also widely begin the practices of abducting human infants and raising them in SCP-2615-B and of planting SCP-2615-A instances to be raised in human society.

Modern Era: 1772 A.D. - Present Day

SCP-2615 have spread across the globe, mostly populating areas with low or no human population. Some major human and SCP-2615 cities act as hubs for SCP-2615/human coexistence. Some SCP-2615 instances are also known to utilize extradimensional spaces for the formation or expansion of nations and to prevent overpopulation.

Most SCP-2615 territories swear allegiance to one of 25 of the original 27 SCP-2615-B nations, with two of the original monarchies being incorporated into the largest monarchy. The existence of these territories has changed the geopolitical status of several baseline nations, with most nations having a lesser amount of territory, and many nations having an increase or decrease of wealth or power based on proximity to and relations with SCP-2615 nations.

Notable widespread integration of anomalies into SCP-2615-B and the daily lives of SCP-2615-A. Some overflow of anomalies into human life and society. The Foundation and most groups of interest still in operation, but with no interest in maintaining the secrecy of the anomalous and having a more relaxed attitude towards anomalies.

Addendum 2:

A common question asked by new members to the SCP-2615 containment project is why we go through the trouble of maintaining the -J article, or why we even made it in the first place. Why not just keep doing the same thing that we do to the public to personnel? The main reason is that it doesn't work. Sure, we can keep telling people that SCP-2615 is all a big myth, but take a second and look around you. Half of the things we contain are what myths are made of. We can keep telling people that SCP-2615 is impossible, but these people work with the impossible every day. As soon as people see what's behind these doors, they begin to wonder what other impossibilities might exist. They begin to wonder about bigfoot, and the bedtime stories their parents used to read them, and the cure for cancer, and they begin to wonder about faeries. And so, we turn faeries into a joke, let people have a laugh at the impossibility of faeries, and leave them thinking just how silly they were to think that they existed. -*Josephine Fujimoto*

Footnotes

1. Organisms possessing five different types of cones in their retina, allowing them to see five primary colors.

SCP-2547

Item #: SCP-2547

Object Class: Keter

Special Containment Procedures: Due to the nature of SCP-2547, effective containment is not possible at this time. Towns determined to be susceptible to SCP-2547 manifestation events are to be monitored via remote surveillance and evacuation of the population is to be attempted if deemed possible. Towns undergoing an event are to be dosed aerially with Class A amnestics at the end of the manifestation event.

Description: SCP-2547 is a pack of approximately 4000 different members of the family Canidae.[1] Members of SCP-2547 do not need food or water. Any attempts to harm, kill or tranquilize a member of SCP-2547 will result in the rest of the group becoming hostile and aggressive. Members of SCP-2547 can be separated from the group and detained, but will disappear the instant they are no longer directly being observed and rejoin SCP-2547. DNA testing has revealed that members of SCP-2547 are genetically identical to human beings.

SCP-2547 only manifests in rural American towns. Affected states include Montana, Wyoming, Utah, Nevada, New Mexico, Arizona, and southern California. The town must have a population of less than 3,000, as well as a reservoir and a church. Manifestations will occur only between June 1 and August 31. For the duration of the event, the local temperature will remain above 32 degrees Celsius, and all local precipitation will cease.

The following is a timeline of SCP-2547 manifestation events.

Immediately Upon Arrival: The town suffers a power outage between midnight and 4 AM. SCP-2547 members form a border around the most densely populated portion of the town and block all attempts at escape. Attempts to enter a vehicle will provoke an attack by SCP-2547.

Three Days After Arrival: Three days after SCP-2547's arrival, all the water in the reservoir will disappear. A male coyote wearing a leather coat altered to accommodate its skeletal structure and a worn wooden crucifix will appear. This entity has been designated SCP-2547-1, though it refers to itself as the Reverend. SCP-2547-1 is capable of both bipedal locomotion and speech.

Time Between SCP-2547-1 Appearance and Departure: SCP-2547-1 will take up residence in the local church and hold regular sermons four times a day. The sermons usually consist of a diatribe on how modern society has forgotten SCP-2547-1 and its siblings, and how they have lost the ability to dream as they once did. SCP-2547-1 ends its sermons by asking if any member of the congregation would like to trade for some water, but does not specify what goods it will take in exchange.

SCP-2547-1 will accept the following as payment: any kind of meat, pepper, flint arrowheads, knives, whips, leather, burlap, belts, the thorns of a saguaro cactus, broken glass, lost teeth, ties, carved sculptures, the corpses of domestic cats, amber, canvas shoes, peyote, chewing tobacco, sexual favors, sulfur, men's button-up shirts, animal skulls, and stories with SCP-2547-1 as the protagonist.[2] SCP-2547-1 will store its payments in the church and assign members of SCP-2547 to guard the pile from theft.

If the payment given is deemed acceptable, SCP-2547-1 will regurgitate 60 to 120 liters of water. If the payment does not fall into any of the above categories, SCP-2547-1 will transform the offender into a member of the Canidae family, who will then join SCP-2547. These altered individuals do not appear to retain memories or intelligence from before their transformation.

Departure: SCP-2547 and -1 will remain until the next full moon after the initial SCP-2547-1 manifestation date, upon which SCP-2547-1 will lead SCP-2547 away from town, using SCP-2547 to transport the goods it obtained.

An excerpt from one of SCP-2547-1's speeches has been provided for reference:

You ask me, who am I. I ask you, where am I? In the beginning there was the word and the word was not a word at all, but a howl. Where am I, in the meat brain, encased in bone, dripping with brine, sizzling with sparks? Where am I in your chemical soup? Am I sacred? Have I been on the cross? Once I was woven into you, all your kind, deep in the pit of yourself from which you pull your wildest tales and strangest desires? I gave you the gift that saved you. I would have been your Eden, I would have tended you as a shepherd his sheep. I taught you all how to lie. And you, though the only way you gibbering sheep of apes survived is through deceit, you have forgotten me!? You have replaced me with a serpent who crawls on the ground!? [SCP-2547 stops, and begins to sob.] I gave you stories. You worshipped me, once. And now you are disgusted. Heretic, you say. No. I am a martyr, like your beloved carpenter. You dare not look upon me, for fear of burning in brimstone. So be it, then. Let me be something that you should truly be repulsed by. You brought this on yourselves. You looked back as Sodom burned.

Interviewer: Agent Miller

Interviewee: SCP-2547-1

Opening Statement: Agent Miller had been stationed in the town of ███████████, Utah, which had been deemed at risk for an SCP-2547-manifestation event. The manifestation event occurred on 6/12/15. Agent Miller had been given 4.5 g of amber and enough water to last him for 3 months. He presented the gift to SCP-2547-1, but requested information in lieu of water.

<Begin Log>

SCP-2547-1: Oh, how beautiful. And look! Look there. A fly, caught in the midst.

Agent Miller: How fitting, given our situation.

SCP-2547-1: Hah! A sense of humor! Oh, I like you. [SCP-2547-1 takes Agent Miller's face in its paws and kisses him. Agent Miller does not respond.] Hm? No? Very well, then. Now, your water.

Agent Miller: I happen to be well stocked with water for now, as it happens.

SCP-2547-1: Cunning you. Perhaps it was good I didn't have you after all - you might have a little too much of me in you for me to be properly in you, it seems. - pardon my pun, of course. It would have been highly embarrassing. But. What boon do you seek of me?

Agent Miller: I'd like to know more about you. What you want. Why you do this. Who you are.

SCP-2547-1: Three questions! Oh, you do know your myths! How delicious. What do I want? Has anyone ever dreamed of you, my beautiful man? I'll bet they have. If so, you'd never want it to stop. Now, why do I do this? To put it in your terms, I'm upping my publicity, of course. The myth field has been taken over by hacks and milquetoasts. I'd like my old hunting grounds to myself. But you can't spread legends the way you used to, not anymore. So my approach has had to be…unorthodox. As to who I am, your kind knows me, all right. You know who I am. Not in the bits of you that do all your numbers and lines, but the parts of you that paint and sing and fuck and leap. I am yours, as you are mine. You know who I am, gorgeous man. All you have to do is look. It's right in front of you, I promise.

<End Log> SCP-2547-1 refused to respond to any further questioning, and left 18 days later. Agent Miller tried to gain more information, but SCP-2547 refused to engage in conversation on any subject except propositioning Agent Miller.

Following Agent Miller's return, Protocol DESERT GRASSROOTS was enacted, which consists of a many-faceted multimedia campaign to produce narratives that involve the SCP-2547-1 entity in some way. Projects created by DESERT GRASSROOTS include:

- A series of children's books centered around modern retelling of Southwestern Native American myths and legends.

- A common street art design depicting a coyote wearing a leather jacket and sunglasses, using a crucifix as a pipe.

- An internet meme template character in the "advice animal" format called Kinky Coyote.

- A television show called *Angels of Dust*, featuring an antagonistic cult with hedonistic beliefs, led by a man calling himself Latrans.

- An interactive fiction game focusing around a pilot, call sign "Coyote One", stranded on an unfamiliar planet after his ship crashed in a desert.

- A modern surrealist art exhibit at the Boston Isabella Gardner museum, which conveys a canid-man hybrid's conversion to an odd religion. The pieces are done entirely in wire sculptures and taxidermy.

- A collaboration album between alternative music artist ███████ ██████ (frontman of alternative-folk band ██ ███) and rap artist ███ ███. The album makes repeated references to an entity called Canis, who represents their primal desires and fears which they must constantly push down and ignore in order to be civilized humans.

Following implementation of Protocol DESERT GRASSROOTS, SCP-2547 manifestation events have decreased in frequency by 30%, but SCP-2547-1 no longer appears to accept stories as payment during events, resulting in a 15% increase in the average number of additions to SCP-2547 per manifestation.

Footnotes

1. Including dogs, foxes, wolves, coyotes, jackals, and dingoes

2. The latter appears to be a favorite of SCP-2547-1, and the highest recorded amounts of water were produced in exchange for such narratives, followed by the volumes produced in exchange for sexual favors.

SCP-2303

Item #: SCP-2303

Object Class: Euclid

SCP-2303, originally intended to serve as the Municipal Office Complex of Ciudad Encrucijada

Special Containment Procedures: Site-885 has been established in proximity to SCP-2303. Foundation activities in the vicinity of the anomaly are to be presented to potential observers as a long-term architectural engineering study. Due to the lack of permanent residents in the area of SCP-2303, Minimum Security Perimeter protocols are in effect.

Monitoring and documentation of SCP-2303 phenomena is to be performed via automated means whenever feasible. In cases where direct observation must be performed, standard memetic hazard safety procedures are to be instituted.

All suspected SCP-2303 phenomena are to be independently investigated and confirmed to the extent possible before being formally entered into the research log.

SCP-2303 research is assigned to Mobile Task Force Phi-9 ("Barqueros"). Members of MTF Phi-9 are currently subject to provisional security clearance authorization. Provisional status will be reevaluated on ██/██/██, per the standard five year probationary period for Special Recruitment personnel.

Description: SCP-2303 is an abandoned high-rise building, located in the ghost city of Ciudad Encrucijada[1], in the Río Negro province of Argentina. SCP-2303 is the apparent focal point for recurring episodes of anomalous information transfer. As observed through specialized methodology and equipment, SCP-2303 is host to a phenomenon wherein concepts and ideas that are not fully realized and never implemented by their originators are communicated to observers in the vicinity. These concepts range widely across the spectrum of human endeavor, and have in the past included proposed artworks, philosophical schools of thought, political systems, scientific theorems, and public works projects.

Information transmitted within SCP-2303 may be observed through a variety of media. Appliances such as antenna-equipped televisions and radios which are powered on but not set to an occupied frequency are capable of receiving and displaying audio and visual information. These typically take the form of short, sporadic bursts of interrelated information, such as sequential scenes from a motion picture, or related tracks from a musical album. SCP-2303 has been outfitted with monitors and recording devices throughout its structure in order to observe this information.

In order to observe more abstract concepts, such as philosophical precepts or hypothetical political movements, direct observation is required. A methodology for discerning the outside influence of SCP-2303 (as opposed to inherent thought processes in the observer) was developed by former Group of Interest GX-5573, a loose collective of academics, artists and amateur researchers from throughout southern Argentina who first encountered the anomaly. This methodology incorporates elements of autohypnosis, meditation techniques developed by indigenous Tehuelche tribespeople, and activities similar to the Spiritualist practices of automatic writing and psychometry.

Individual works and concepts encountered within SCP-2303 are observable for a time period of between three days and five weeks. Information presented within SCP-2303 will become less contextualized and coherent from occurrence to occurrence, until the unifying concept decays and is no longer observable.

The manifestation of ideas presented in SCP-2303 do not appear to be linked chronologically to their originators. While concepts imagined within the past thirty years comprise the majority of observed data, older ideas have been documented, in some cases originating hundreds of years prior to observation.

Addendum 2303.1 - Concepts Observed Within SCP-2303

Floors 1-12: Artistic Works

Location Observed	Description	Notes
Floor Eight, Hallway	Inmate art exhibit, Ferguson Prison	Correctional officers at Ferguson Prison in Midway, Texas, considered staging a public exhibition of paintings by inmates as a means of improving morale and performing local community outreach. Most of the works submitted were painted by ███████████, a particularly notorious offender convicted of multiple counts of murder.
Floor Three, Room 32	Sequels to *The Last Temptation of Christ*	Two concepts were observed in this location, but were interrelated. The first was a planned novel by author William Styron following up on the events of the original work by Nikos Kazantzakis, told from the perspective of Judas. The second was an adaptation of the proposed Styron project into a film directed by filmmaker Terence Malick. While no evidence exists that Styron ever advanced beyond discussing the idea, the film adaptation apparently progressed to the point of obtaining a commitment from actor Harvey Keitel to reprise the role of Judas before the project was abandoned.
Floor Five, ceiling crawlspace	Alternate soundtrack to *A Serbian Film*	This occurrence consisted of one hour and fifty-seven minutes of music intended to serve as a soundtrack to the motion picture *A Serbian Film*, recorded by industrial noise act Pharmakon. This was apparently intended to broaden the film's appeal to American audiences. The film was ultimately scored by Serbian musician Wikluh Sky.
Floor Eleven, Room 8	Comedic spoken-word performance, 2011 Hajj	A group of students at the International Islamic University in Islamabad considered holding a stand-up comedy festival at the Miqat Qarn al-Manazil prior to the 2011 Hajj as an attempt to create positive coverage in Western media outlets. Several established performers had been committed to the project before it was aborted.

Floors 13-19: Religion and Philosophy

Location Observed	Description	Notes
Floor Seventeen, Room 12	*Treatise on the Importance of Self-Extinction*	This work, written by an unknown scholar, consisted of a discussion between eight characters citing the works of Aristotle, Thomas Aquinas, Avicenna, and several lesser-known figures in philosophical thought, making an argument for the moral imperative of suicide. The work concludes with each character committing suicide in turn. The scholarly citations and style of writing suggests that the work was considered during the ninth century AD by an author residing in Moorish Cordoba, making this entry the oldest observed unimplemented concept found within SCP-2303 to date.
Floor Nineteen, Room 32	Church of the Twelfth Prophet	A nascent religious movement before ultimately disbanding in 2004, this doctrine held that the Mahdi, a messianic figure prominent in Islam, is also the twelfth Guru of Sikhism[2]. ████████████, the individual claiming to be the eponymous Twelfth Prophet, was provisionally classified as a Person of Interest due to suspected anomalous phenomena associated with their activities before disappearing in January of 2005.
Floor Fourteen, North Elevator Shaft	Brewsterism	This phenomenon was a school of intellectual thought, discussed among a group of doctoral students at the University of Salzburg, proposing the infallibility of the writings of Harold Brewster, an unemployed Irish university professor residing in the Weimar Republic during the 1920s. Post-observational verification of Brewster's papers reveal several anachronistic commentaries on modern fields of science, such as biomolecular engineering, m-theory, and exoplanetary astronomy. Brewster's papers also contain lengthy, nonsensical exhortations against activities such as creating music, riding bicycles and sleeping. The majority of Brewster's writings are suspected to have been destroyed immediately prior to the abandonment of Brewsterism by its

		proponents.
Floor Eighteen, Air Vent Between Rooms 3 and 9	*Sixth Meditation on the Actualization of Salvation*	Extant materials related to this concept consist of 255 wheatpasted flyers, distributed throughout urban areas in the Kitchener, Ontario metropolitan region. The only information on the flyers consisted of the phrase "Sixth Meditation on the Actualization of Salvation," an address of a private residence in Bujumbura, Burundi, and an appointed time of 2300 hours, 29 July, 2005. Based on observational data, this meeting was intended to be a gathering of unknown persons, with the intent of generating a thoughtform entity through anomalous means[3]. Flyers were intended to be posted in eighteen additional cities in fifteen countries before this project was abandoned.

Floors 20-27: Public Works and Large Scale Coordinated Projects

Location Observed	Description	Notes
Floor Twenty-Six, Room 21	Proposed Australian space program	Confirmed by examination of classified documents, several officials in the Australian Ministry of Industry, Innovation and Science proposed a multi-billion dollar investment in a new space exploration initiative, culminating in an interstellar satellite mission. Detailed information of this proposal ceases sometime around the launch of a research mission bound for the Saturnian moon of Iapetus.
Floor Twenty-One, Room 6B	Low-cost cryonics initiative	A crowdfunded project was considered by ███████████, a high-profile startup investor in Scottsdale, Arizona, to construct several low-cost facilities designed to house large quantities of cryopreserved human remains. This project was intended to increase public awareness, acceptance, and adoption of cryonics as a funerary practice.
Floor Twenty, Main Utility Access Hall	Karnali River Dam	A hydroengineering firm based in the United Kingdom was considering a proposal to construct a massive dam project on the Karnali River in Nepal. Despite no evidence that the project ever progressed beyond internal planning discussions, the concept engendered several large protests in

		Nepali rural areas, as well as a speech in the Indian Parliament condemning the project as a "theft of resources that cannot go unanswered."
Floor Twenty-Three, Lobby	Zambezi Superdeep Borehole	Sometime during the early 1970s, Mozambican officials were presented with a plan for a deep drilling project intended to penetrate the Earth's crust 50 km offshore in the Indian Ocean, as part of an experimental new method for hydrocarbon and mineral extraction. Of note is the fact that the proposed site would eventually be used for a similar project in connection with SCP-2798.

Floors 28-31: Science

Location Observed	Description	Notes
Floor Twenty-Nine, Cafeteria	Argus Radio Observatory System	This proposal was discussed in three separate meetings between entrepreneur Jeff Bezos and SpaceX COO Gwynne Shotwell, centering around a prospective $50 billion investment in a network of omnidirectional radio telescopes dedicated to searching for evidence of extraterrestrial civilizations, to be known collectively as the Argus Radio Observatory System. The project was not discussed again after the third meeting between Bezos and Shotwell, documented to have occurred on the campus of the Lawrence Livermore National Laboratory.
Floor Thirty, Room 13	Engineered anti-syphilis phage introduction	In 2011, researchers at Moscow Medical Academy claimed to have developed a species of bacteriophage that would eliminate all forms of syphilis. In a meeting with Kremlin officials later that year, the lead project researcher proposed to introduce this bacteriophage "into the wild" throughout Russia as a public health measure. This plan was rejected by the Kremlin three weeks later.
Floor Twenty-Seven, Room 1	Superconducting Super Collider	This particle accelerator complex, proposed in the 1970s in the United States, would have been the world's largest particle accelerator, approximately twice as large as the Large Hadron Collider and projected to generate approximately three times its energy. This project was formally cancelled by the United

		States Congress in 1993.

Floor 32: CLASSIFIED

Location Observed	Description	Notes
Floor Thirty-Two, Grand Hall	*The Man at the Threshold*	DATA RESTRICTED TO LEVEL 5 CLEARANCE

Addendum 2303.2 - MTF Phi-9 Introductory Statement

FROM: Rojas, Aurelio
TO: Guest4939
RE: <none>
Attachment: HANDBOOK_PHI_9.pdf, securityapp.pdf, HR_rates_plans.xls, OPEN_THIS_LAST.xyx, DONT_OPEN.aad

Let's get this thing out of the way. This is Phi-9, and most of us were inducted to the Foundation from outside. You are joining us with none of our history.

That's good.

You're a Barquero now. That means you ferry this stuff to wherever the hell it goes after it's gone. The bosses above told you to document this and research it and what have you. Don't worry, we're going to do plenty of that.

But really, you're here to watch these things in the tower go away and disappear. To make sure they go away and disappear. Eduardo calls them dreams but he's an asshole and not to be trusted. You'll find that out soon.

All the formal stuff and the manuals are there. You'll read them eight times without me needing to tell you. Oh man, the culture shock. Most of you aren't from the Southern Hemisphere. We do things different. Yeah, read the manuals. Then close those and listen to me.

You're going to be in that tower soon. Exciting, right? They tell me people ask to be here. You're going to read the manuals no matter what I tell you, so you're going to be on your guard, so much that you think you'll never let it down again.

Bullshit. One day, and it's going to be soon, I promise you, you're going to think "hey, that one's a pretty good idea, bring that one out, man." I know you are. It happens a lot. It happened to me on the top floor. I thought I knew better than this madhouse that we all were so smitten by. I told everyone that we needed to save something from here. We should pull it back out I said, this is just too beautiful. And it was. We all dropped to our knees to see it, even after it started doing what it did.

When it was over, I ran as fast as I could into the night to find anyone that could help us put things back. There was a lot to clean up.

Here's your first order, don't ask about the other Barqueros, from before this was an official outfit. There's eight of us left from the top floor thing. There were a lot more before.

Here's your other first order. You leave that shit in the tower. Every single thing you see in there is a painted corpse. That's because it's a grave. All of it stays in there to rot and die, no matter what, or I put the bullet in your head myself. I look out for my people, and you're one of mine now.

Welcome aboard, Barquero.

ROJAS

Footnotes

1. Despite its intended purpose as a regional financial center planned by the Argentine government in the 1970s, Ciudad Encrucijada was never fully inhabited, and was abandoned soon after construction of the city center was completed. The Argentinian Ministry of Modernization reported a population of zero for Ciudad Encrucijada in 1978.

2. Note that mainstream Sikhism holds that only eleven Gurus exist.

3. Though unconfirmed, these methods are believed to be derived from those used in the creation of SCP-1984-1.

SCP-4028

Item #: SCP-4028

Object Class: Keter

Fig 1.1: A depiction of SCP-4028 (from the cover of a 1827 British edition of *Don Quixote*).

Special Containment Procedures: The development of effective containment procedures for SCP-4028 is ongoing. Meanwhile, personnel are to focus on the expungement of all canonical deviations in fiction caused by SCP-4028. To accomplish this, the following measures are in place:

- A Foundation-operated bot (I/O-ISMETA) is to monitor academic journals focused on Western literature and flag articles discussing texts deviating from canons for review.

- A Foundation-operated bot (I/O-MANDELA) is to monitor online fiction communities and flag discussions regarding texts deviating from canons for review.

- Texts which deviate from established literary canons are to be reviewed by MTF Rho-1 ("The Professors") to determine whether or not these deviations constitute evidence of alterations by SCP-4028.

- When an altered text is identified, a joint operation conducted by MTF Rho-1 ("The Professors"), MTF Mu-4 ("Debuggers"), and MTF Gamma-5 ("Red Herrings") is to expunge all knowledge (digital, physical, and anecdotal) of these texts from public records.

- When feasible, altered texts are to be restored to their unaltered state. Otherwise, these texts are to be destroyed.

Description: SCP-4028 is Alonso Quixano, the protagonist of Miguel de Cervantes' 17th century Spanish novel, *El Ingenioso Hidalgo Don Quijote de la Mancha* (*The Ingenious Nobleman Sir Quixote of La Mancha*, or *Don Quixote*). In *Don Quixote*, Alonso Quixano is a Spanish noble (or *hidalgo*) who goes mad from reading chivalric romances. He proclaims himself a knight-errant and takes the name Don Quixote de la Mancha, recruiting a simple farmer (Sancho Panza) to act as his loyal squire. *Don Quixote* was published by Cervantes in two parts (the first in 1605, and the second in 1615); it is widely considered to be one of the most influential works in Western literature.

SCP-4028 is a sapient metafictional construct capable of inhabiting and altering fictional texts narratively adjacent to the one it occupies. Adjacency is determined via characters or settings shared between texts. SCP-4028 alters stories it enters to more closely fit its ideals of knightly conduct. This includes defending those it perceives as helpless, striking down those it perceives as wicked, and extolling the virtues of romantic chivalry.

Addendum 4028.1: Examples of Altered Texts

ORIGINAL TEXT	ALTERATIONS
A 1845 copy of the *New York Tribune* containing the poem, *The Raven*.	After the seventh refrain, Alonso Quixano arrives on horseback and strikes the raven down with an axe. The remainder of the poem is a debate between the narrator and Alonso regarding who is lovelier: the narrator's lost Lenore, or Alonso's beloved Dulcinea. It concludes with a fist-fight.[1]
An 1847 English edition of *A Christmas Carol*.	After Ebeneezer Scrooge arrives at the churchyard, Alonso Quixano charges the Ghost of Christmas Yet to Come on horseback, striking it down. Alonso then carries Ebeneezer home atop an exhausted Rocinante.[2] The story continues as before, with Ebeneezer awakening in his bed as a changed man. An additional paragraph at the end mentions the world's gratitude to the mysterious knight who 'slew Death itself'.
An 1876 English edition of *Memoirs of a Woman of Pleasure* (or *Fanny Hill*).	Fanny writes to 'Madame' about the mysterious knight who arrived on horseback and struck down a brothel moments before it lured her into its doors. The stranger then gave her a sack of gold acquired from "a miserly fellow who had no more need of it". She used this money to establish an orphanage and school for poor and vulnerable children such as herself. The remainder of the book consists of Fanny explaining the pleasures and meaning behind various types of flower arrangements (complete with illustrations).
An 1881 French edition of *Justine, or the*	As the story begins, Alonso Quixano joins the twelve year old Justine; he accompanies her until the novel's

Misfortunes of Virtue.	end. All encounters which previously resulted in Justine's torture, assault, and/or rape are now resolved by Alonso preemptively striking down the responsible parties as soon as they appear. Justine eventually re-unites with her sister, Juliette. Alonso strikes down a lightning bolt intended for them both, then challenges the narrator to a duel. The story hastily concludes with both sisters receiving a large inheritance and living happily ever after.
A 1956 English edition of *The Fellowship of the Ring*.	Alonso Quixano appears at the Council of Elrond, where he suggests a joust to determine who should carry the ring. After this idea is dismissed by Gandalf, Alonso states that he will "finish this fool errand myself, then". He takes the ring and rides to Mordor, striking down all evil-doers he encounters along the way. Once there, he returns the ring to Sauron ("as it is your property, and therefore yours by right") and challenges him to a duel. Sauron accepts, and is immediately struck down.
A 1982 English edition of *The Dark Tower: The Gunslinger*.	Immediately after the opening line ('The man in Black fled across the Desert, and the Gunslinger followed'), Alonso appears on horseback. He overtakes Walter (the man in Black), incapacitates him with a blow from his sword, then drags him back to Roland (the Gunslinger). Once Walter awakens, he is forced to duel Roland honorably (under Alonso's watchful eye). Roland strikes Walter down. The remainder of the novel consists of vignettes wherein Alonso instructs Roland on how to be a virtuous knight, including taking Jake on as his squire and fighting evil throughout the wastes.
A 1997 English edition of *Harry Potter and the Philosopher's Stone*.	When Rubeus Hagrid arrives to tell Harry that he has been accepted into Hogwarts, Alonso arrives on horseback and strikes the half-giant down. Alonso then explains to Harry that giants, wizards, and sorcerers all traffic with the Devil and must be avoided at any cost. The remainder of the novel consists of Harry living a life of patient penitence with the Dursleys, who have been inspired by Alonso's example to become kind and virtuous guardians.

Addendum 4028.2: Discovery and Designation

Evidence for the existence of SCP-4028 was first noted by Foundation personnel in 2005 after the discovery of a manuscript previously thought lost (*Historia del Huérfano*, or *The Orphan's Story*). Written between 1608 and 1615 by Martín de León y Cárdenas (a Malagan-born monk), *The Orphan's Story* features Alonso Quixano as a supporting character. He criticizes the narrative for failing to conform to the virtues of romantic chivalry, spends several pages extolling these virtues, then challenges Sir Francis Drake to a duel.[3]

Researchers could not determine whether the incongruity between Alonso Quixano's appearance in *The Orphan's Story* and *Don Quixote* constituted an anomaly or a collaboration between their respective authors. This led to the involvement of the Pataphysics Department (a fictitious department created for the purposes of investigating, counteracting, and containing allegorical and/or metafictional anomalies) to settle the dispute.

After significant debate, the use of SCP-423 (a sapient metafictional construct capable of entering and exploring textual narratives) to determine whether Alonso Quixano's appearance in *The Orphan's Story* was anomalous was authorized. Notably, Dr. Pierre Menard (a leading scholar of *Don Quixote* and the director of the Pataphysics Department at the time) requested that his opposition to this motion be noted in SCP-4028's documentation.[4]

SCP-423 was introduced to a journal and briefed on his task via hand-written notes by Agent O'Hara:

SCP-423 JOURNAL EXCERPT

DATE: 21/08/2005
INTERVIEWER: Agent O'Hara

Hello.

SCP-423, you're going to be entering a 17th century Spanish manuscript entitled The Orphan's Story. We need you to determine if one of the characters in it was inserted anomalously.

Okay. I don't know Spanish, though. What's the book about?

We've translated a copy to English for you. It's about a Granada-born orphan who travels to the Spanish empire in the Americas.

Neat. So, what character am I investigating?

Alonso Quixano. He appears near the end, in a segment where Sir Francis Drake launches a failed attack on Puerto Rico.

Okay.

Wait.

Alonso Quixano?

That is correct.

Alonso Quixano.

Yes.

Don Quixote.

Yes.

***The* Don Quixote.**

Correct.

You're sending me in after Don Quixote.

Is there a problem?

I... look, not to be a dick, but do you have any idea who the heck this guy is?

You're not sending me after some two-bit noir cut-out or a hoighty-toighty meta-vore. This is *the Man of La Mancha*. His fourth wall breaks have got fourth wall breaks. He's got fan-fiction about himself in his own story, which itself is fan-fiction of a story that doesn't even exist. He basically wrote the book on metafiction. Like, literally — it's his book.

So, can you do this?

Jeez. Yeah. Just, uh — don't blame me if things go squirrely, okay?

Just be careful.

After entering an English translation of *The Orphan's Story*, researchers noted that all reference to SCP-4028 within it disappeared. This change occurred simultaneously across all known copies of the manuscript. Immediately thereafter, SCP-423 returned to his journal and re-initiated contact with Agent O'Hara.

SCP-423 JOURNAL EXCERPT

DATE: 23/08/2005
INTERVIEWER: Agent O'Hara

Crap.

Crap crap *crap*.

CRAP.

SCP-423, what happened?

I think I ticked him off. I think, uh — look, you might want to call some people and tell them that we could have a serious metanarrative crisis on our hands.

Please explain.

So, first he thinks I'm some sort of evil wizard, right? I tell him I'm not. I tell him I was sent here to figure out what his deal is — find out if he's in the wrong book. I tell him I was sent by the Foundation, this big organization that investigates anomalies like him. Then he sits down and gets real quiet for a while. And, uh.

And?

He asks me if the Foundation upholds the virtues of knightly chivalry. And...

What did you tell him?

Look, it's not like you guys aren't good, sometimes — but sometimes you're, y'know, not so good? Sometimes you're kind of bad. It's complicated, okay? And that's what I told him. 'It's complicated'. I kept trying to explain that, but, uh, this is not a guy who 'gets' complicated. So after a while, he just stands, draws this busted up sword, says some stuff, and I just — I just ran. I just ran as fast as I could.

What did he say?

You need to call your people. You need to call them and tell them he's coming.

Fred. What did he say?

He said you sound like giants.

One week after this event, SCP-4028 began to manifest in multiple works throughout Western literature. SCP-4028 has since been designated as anomalous.[5]

Footnotes

1. Dulcinea's true name was Aldonza Lorenzo. She was a peasant farm-girl who never even knew Alonso existed.

2. An aging, long-suffering steed.

3. *Imbécil.*

4. Better to let sleeping dogs lie.

5. I warned them. There is no reasoning with that stubborn old fool.

SCP-3353

Item #: SCP-3353

Object Class: Keter

Mushroom ring produced at the conclusion of an SCP-3353 event.

Special Containment Procedures: Foundation historians specializing in European folklore are to maintain a list of numerically-significant dates to predict future SCP-3353 manifestations. Locations that have been confirmed affected by SCP-3353 manifestations are to be investigated at least twice monthly, as per dates noted on the predictive list.

Should SCP-3353 manifest during a monitoring session, Foundation agents are to patrol the area and intercept any passersby who approach the location of manifestation too closely. Amnestics may be administered as necessary.

A disinformation team of at least ten researchers is to monitor social media outlets for reports of SCP-3353 sightings. SCP-3353 is to be explained as a low-attention public artistic project involving fairy tale enthusiasts attempting to "make people's lives a little more magical!" To aid with this cover story, five SCP-3353 disinformation team members are to maintain several active artistic blog accounts, which regularly post a variety of mundane art content in addition to recipes and crafts instructions for making non-anomalous versions of the apples and desserts produced by SCP-3353.

Apples recovered from SCP-3353 events are to be kept for analysis in low-priority storage. Should the apples spoil, they can be disposed of in non-anomalous waste containers.

Description: SCP-3353 refers to a recurring anomalous phenomenon, which initially manifests with the spontaneous appearance of an intangible apple tree[1] within a public garden or park area. SCP-3353 events occur most commonly in the United Kingdom and Ireland, typically beginning at midnight and concluding after three hours. (Additional SCP-3353 sightings have been reported by social media accounts originating in Australia and Japan, but these cases are currently unconfirmed.)

Following the appearance of the apple tree, several apples will manifest beneath it. These apples appear non-anomalous, with the exception of not displaying on digital device screens when photographed or videotaped. Closer inspection will reveal the words "Tell me a secret" etched in neat handwriting into the skin of the apples, as if carved with a small knife.

Should a human individual voice a personal statement while holding an apple produced by SCP-3353, there is a chance that the apple will vanish and be replaced by a small dessert (biscuits, tarts, or small cakes). Desserts produced through this effect are universally enjoyed by any individuals who consume them, regardless of existing taste preferences, and appear otherwise non-anomalous. It is further noted that SCP-3353 desserts tend to spoil at a quicker rate than non-anomalous counterparts.

In rare cases, individuals who handle an apple produced by SCP-3353 but attempt to hide it on their person or otherwise refuse to speak to it will grow drowsy, eventually falling into a deep sleep for several hours. This effect seems to result in extreme disorientation upon awakening, but no lasting harm. Apples that were not handled during the SCP-3353 manifestation will revert to non-anomalous variants (with no etching) at the conclusion of the event.

At the conclusion of the SCP-3353 manifestation, the apple tree will be replaced with a ring of mushrooms[2]. The mushrooms produced are consistently local species and possess no anomalous qualities.

Addendum SCP-3353-1: The first recorded case of SCP-3353 manifestation occurred on 03/23/2013, when two Foundation personnel patrolling a privately-owned park during their routine duties noticed the unusual apple tree associated with the presence of SCP-3353. The personnel approached the tree, noting that both it and the surrounding apples on the ground did not display on the surveillance cameras.

After contacting the nearest Foundation Site, Researcher Dominic Harris (Doctor of Humanities, University of Cambridge) was authorized to further investigate the anomaly. He proceeded to interact with three apples[3] until the following results were produced (spoken words present in italics):

"I tell my mother that I like her cooking, but I really don't."	No change noted.

"I'm embarrassed by not knowing the difference between vegan and vegetarian, even though my girlfriend is vegetarian."	Apple cracked in half, and transformed into a small cupcake.
"When I was younger I smashed my friend's toy car, because I secretly wanted them to pay more attention to me."	No change noted.
"If I can get away with it, I won't bathe for a few days in a row or I'll only wash my body and not my hair because it feels like a chore and unnecessary too."	No change noted.
"One time I mispronounced a word and people laughed at me, so I went home and looked up lists of mispronounced words and practiced them."	Apple transformed into a Manchester tart.
"I shave the hair on my knuckles every month."	No change noted.
"I feel really awkward when I eat too slow or can't finish a meal in public, so I pretend that I like home cooking to eat alone as often as possible."	Apple transformed into a Manchester tart.

Researcher Harris later reported that he felt that the exchange was "not a fair trade, all things considered" and that the anomaly itself seemed to be "more of a prank than anything else".

The SCP-3353 research team is currently discussing how to assign personnel stationed in the United Kingdom for further investigation.

Footnotes

1. Typically measuring 2-3 meters in height and as a result relatively inconspicuous in appearance

2. Commonly called a "fairy circle", "elf circle", or "fairy ring" in Western Europe

3. Researcher Harris has attested to the truthfulness of all recorded statements.

SCP-1918

Item #: SCP-1918

Object Class: Euclid

Image No #: 1918-A

Entity interaction with D-2934..

Image captured 08/31/10

Special Containment Procedures: Entrances to SCP-1918-2 have been secured and monitored with constant video surveillance as of 03/05/██. The sewage facility containing 3 entrances has been quarantined by Foundation personnel and the entrances themselves have been sealed. Workers previously employed at the facility have been issued amnestics and replaced with Foundation personnel. All other entrances have been permanently sealed with cement.

SCP-1918-2 is visible via seismic imaging, though the location may not be physically breached as per agreed upon Foundation escalation prevention protocols.

Description: SCP-1918 is an object of unknown composition located in SCP-1918-2. It appears to be a plastic mold attached to a metallic rod, and is usually found moving between hallways in 1918-2. SCP-1918 moves on its own volition, although it does not appear to separate from the ground at any time. The object leans in the direction it travels in, and moves at a set speed of 5 kph. The object applies moderate force to the surfaces it moves across, leaving a faint trail. SCP-1918 at times communicates using these carvings.

SCP-1918-2 is the designation for the area containing SCP-1918. The area is located in a cavity 20 meters beneath ██████, Maine. SCP-1918-2 is similar in appearance to electrical substations located in the region. There are 18 identical rooms in SCP-1918-2, or 9 compound rooms. Rooms are differentiated between a '1' room and a '2' room by crude carvings on the floors outside of the individual rooms. SCP-1918-2 is symmetrical, with .5 meter wide paths circling each compound room. The only deviations to this construction are the location of entrances on the sides of each individual room, which vary randomly while the facility is active. A visual representation of SCP-1918-2 is available as Image No #: 1918-B.

Access to SCP-1918-2 is non-euclidean; entrances to this location tend to be kilometres apart from one another. There are currently 9 known entrances, including 5 sewage grates, 3 utility shafts located in a sewage facility, and 1 toilet. Exit from the facility is not believed to be possible, although evidence in Testing Log 1918.14 suggests this possibility.

Hallways in the facility are completely devoid of light. Any light produced is absorbed via an unknown mechanism; due to this, exploration must be performed via memorization of the facility interior and touch. Sound behaves abnormally within SCP-1918-2 while an event is active; an audible echo can be heard five (5) seconds after a sound (inaudible) is actually produced.

The floors of rooms in SCP-1918-2 contain residues which are believed to originate from bodily fluids of individuals trapped in the area.

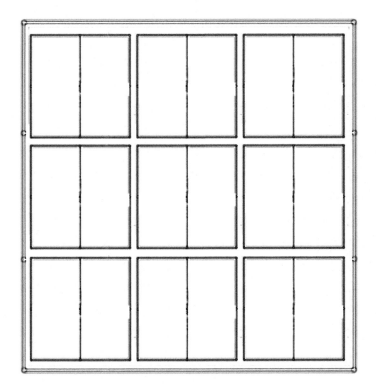

Visual representation depicting the layout of the facility, 1918-2.

It is not currently known whether or not SCP-1918 and SCP-1918-2 are separate or identical manifestations as attempts to remove SCP-1918 from SCP-1918-2 have been largely unsuccessful.

When a human or canine subject enters the central room it will become illuminated, and SCP-1918-2 will manifest. SCP-1918 will enter the room and move across the floor, leaving in its trail a message either reading "Tik Tak Tow" or "Memoree", maintaining a consistent speed and leaving immediately after the message has been inscribed. If the subject attempts to exit the room before this, the room will return to its dormant state, with the subject and any of its possessions disappearing immediately.

1. *"Tik Tak Tow"* | The object moves to each "1" room, leaving behind "X" markings on the floors if the room is not already marked with an "O" in a manner similar to a game of "Tic Tac Toe". How a subject is meant to accomplish making a mark or understand this process is unknown, as no aides are given.

2. *"Memoree"* | Upon exiting the room the subject is rendered unconscious by blunt force, presumably from SCP-1918. The subject regains consciousness in a random section of the facility. Success is marked by finding a "1" room identical to the central room. This event seems to possess a time limit, as the subject is pursued by SCP-1918 throughout the halls of the facility. The subject "wins" by marking the correct room with an "O".

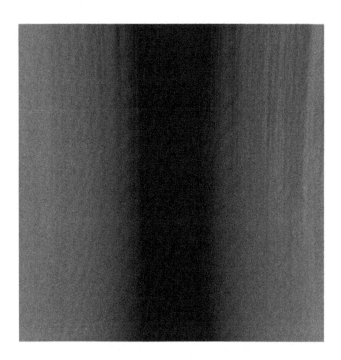

Computer generated image depicting a hallway structure in SCP-1918-2.

Entering a "2" room causes SCP-1918-2 to enter a dormant state, and what is assumed to be the death of the subject participating.

If the subject is successful, SCP-1918 will present itself in the room that the subject is currently in. SCP-1918 will then inscribe "new game" on the floor and repeat the process with a new event. If the subject is unsuccessful, SCP-1918-2 will simply revert to its dormant state with the subject participating in the previous event disappearing.

History: SCP-1918-2 came to the attention of the Foundation after the disappearance of four utility workers in ███, a small town (pop. 226) in Maine. Numerous reports were filed to the local sheriff's department of a "metallic scraping" beneath the ground, most commonly audible near sewage grates.

Addendum A: Recordings from testing event coordinated on 08/31/10.

Close

D-Class subject is equipped with an earpiece, headlamp, and a chest mounted camera with a live feed to Researchers. Subject is then instructed to enter entrance 2.

D-2934: Okay, so where's this tunnel taking me?

Researcher Sanders: You have been briefed. Continue.

D-2934: Okay, so when I get there I do this game and I leave? Why can't I do that other thing you guys sent up Paul to do earlier?

Researcher Sanders: You have been selected for your expert knowledge of the subject. Where are you located currently?

D-2934: Tunnel stopped, I mean the concrete part. It's a big ole' cave, uh, I can see a hole on the end.

Researcher Sanders: Enter the hole.

D-2934: You sure about that? Shouldn't y'all be sending in robots or something?

Researcher Sanders: Would you like to terminate testing, D-2934?

D-2934: Oh yeah, alright, nah that's alright, yeah I'm headed in. Hell, this is kind of exciting I guess.

Audio and video feed useless as expected during travel in halls. D-2934 moves through darkness before the room is illuminated, and SCP-1918 becomes visible in what is assumed to be the central room.

D-2934: Hey who turned on the lights? Hot damn, what the hell is that thing!? Hey there, hey you guys see this? Hear me? Is that the thing?

D-2934: It's… oh well ya'll are seein' this right? What's, oh, Tic Tac Toe, haha, what? – hey where's that thing going? I mean I know where it's goin' but–

Researcher Sanders: Please begin the protocol. You have been briefed. Please move quickly.

Video feed black. Scraping against metal can be heard.

Video and audio effective after four minutes.

D-2934: Hah! Beat 'im to it! So I mark an "O" right? I'm on top left right now, felt the walls, remember it like my hand. Hah. Ya'll can hear me right? HEY, YOU GUYS THERE?

Researcher Sanders: Yes.

Subject produces marker and marks the floor. SCP-1918 appears in the doorway.

D-2934: Hey ya'll didn't tell me about this, what's it doin'?

SCP-1918 remains in the doorway.

Researcher Sanders: This behavior is currently undocumented. Your cooperation is appreciated.

D-2934: The hell does that mean?

SCP-1918 remains in the doorway for four more minutes.

D-2934: Hey, motherfucker, you gonna let me by?

SCP-1918 tilts slightly left and right.

D-2934: Sore fuckin' loser, it's just one "O" go mark off another one!

SCP-1918 leaves the doorway back into the halls.

Researcher Sanders: Please continue.

After a course of 20 minutes the event is completed, with D-2934 successful.

D-2934: Hot damn, that means I won. Sucker didn't even get one box!

Researcher Sanders: Please await the arrival of SCP-1918.

D-2934: The fuck you mean?

SCP-1918 enters the room, inscribing "cheat", "new game", and then "memoree" on the floor of the room.

D-2934: Okay. Okay. What the fuck-ever Pez Dispenser motherfucker.

D-2934 is incapacitated upon exiting the room. Video feed resumes four hours later, although scraping can be heard continually.

Earpiece and microphone appear to be damaged or lost as audio is no longer audible.

Video appears shaky as D-2934 enters a room, most likely due to severe head trauma.

D-2934 exits the room, moving quickly.

After 12 minutes D-2934 enters another room and appears to clap and rub his hands together.

D-2934 approaches the center of the room. D-2934 appears to make a questioning gesture.

D-2934 paces the room for 3 minutes.

D-2934 approaches a rusted pipe visible on one of the sides of the room.

D-2934 moves his wrist along the pipe, drawing blood, and leans against the wall holding said wrist for a short time.

D-2934 enters a crouching position at the center of the room and smears his wrist repeatedly in a circular pattern.

D-2934 returns to standing position, removes jumpsuit and wraps it around the wrist.

SCP-1918 appears in the doorway. D-2934 remains still.

SCP-1918 inscribes "cheat" and "new game" into the floor and moves to the doorway, then turns around and wobbles left and right slightly.

D-2934 grasps his right forearm with his left hand and extends his middle finger at SCP-1918.

SCP-1918 approaches D-2934.

D-2934 moves to the corner of the room quickly and produces a pipe. D-2934 rushes at SCP-1918 and begins beating it repeatedly in the 'head' with the end of the pipe.

The 'head' of SCP-1918 appears to crack and bleed in certain areas as D-2934 makes contact with the pipe. What appears to be grey matter can be seen falling out of the head of SCP-1918 before video feed ends.

Video feed resumes, although view is fixed continually at the ceiling of the room. (Five hours)

D-2934's head becomes visible, appearing to lean forward to look into the camera, before leaning backwards out of view.

Video feed ends two hours afterwards.

71

SCP-1000

Item #: SCP-1000

Object Class: Keter

Still from unverified amateur footage

<u>Special Containment Procedures:</u> All media reports related to SCP-1000 are to be examined for potential verifiability. All organizations and individuals investigating SCP-1000's existence are to be kept under surveillance by Mobile Task Force Zeta-1000 and discredited or administered amnestics. All physical signs of SCP-1000's existence must be retrieved and kept in Foundation custody, and replaced with decoy items if necessary. Alleged sightings of SCP-1000 must always be investigated by MTF Zeta-1000, however trivial the claim.

Absolutely no contact with wild or captive instances of SCP-1000 is allowed without prior approval by Director Jones. Any interaction between SCP-1000 and humans, including Foundation personnel, must be reported to Director Jones immediately.

<u>Description</u>: SCP-1000 is a nocturnal, omnivorous ape, classified in the *Hominini* branch along with genera *Pan* and *Homo*. Adults range in size from 1.5 to 3 m (5 to 10 ft) in height, and weigh between 90 and 270 kg (200 - 600 lbs). They have grey, brown, black, red, and occasionally white fur. They possess large eyes with good vision, a pronounced brow ridge, and a sagittal crest on the forehead similar to that of the gorilla, but present in both sexes. Their intelligence is on par with that of *Pan troglodytes* (the common chimpanzee).

SCP-1000 evolved alongside *Homo sapiens*, existing contemporaneously with proto-humans and humans in large numbers until 10,000-15,000 years ago, when an extinction event eliminated all but 1-5% of their population. This event was triggered by SCP-1000 contracting an anomalous "pseudo-disease" classified as SCP-1000-f1. This disease is passed on at the genetic level and affects every present-day instance of SCP-1000. The majority of SCP-1000 instances are born immune to the effect; those who are not born immune quickly die.

The effect of SCP-1000-f1 is as follows: Any hominid (including humans, chimpanzees, bonobos, and non-immune instances of SCP-1000) that directly or indirectly observes any instance of SCP-1000 has a minimum 2% chance of being instantly killed through anomalous means via permanent cessation of brain function. This percentage is cumulative, and the longer a human views SCP-1000, the higher the chance of instantaneous death increases, at a rate of +1% chance per 20 minutes of viewing. This effect varies between individual members of SCP-1000's species, with some individuals carrying a 'death chance' of 90%. The effect is also produced by dead individuals, though small fur samples do not exhibit the effect.

Known means of preventing this effect are small-scale only and include [REDACTED] (see attached documentation; Level 3 clearance required).

Because of SCP-1000's close relation to humanity, it is considered likely that SCP-1000-f1 could eventually transfer to human carriers. Any instance of SCP-1000 finding its way to a major population center could constitute an █-class end of the world scenario with a minimum death toll of [REDACTED] and possible extinction of humanity. Fortunately, SCP-1000 appears to instinctively avoid human contact.

It is not currently feasible to exterminate SCP-1000 entirely.

The highest known population concentrations of SCP-1000 are at present located in the Pacific Northwest region of North America and the Himalayan Mountain range in Asia. As of █/█/███, these populations remain extant. SCP-1000's presence and [DATA EXPUNGED] have also been documented within the past 5 years on every continent. All known significant populations of SCP-1000 located near human population centers have been eliminated.

SCP-1000 came to the attention of the Foundation via contact by Doctor Franz M███████ in 14██ with the Children of the Sun, who identified themselves as outcast members of the Serpent's Hand. This group has since been completely destroyed by the Foundation, due to their reluctance to surrender information about SCP-1000, SCP-███, and SCP-███ (since reclassified as SCP-1000-███ and SCP-1000-███). Remaining members have either joined the Foundation, or have gone into hiding, presumably as members of the Serpent's Hand. Weapons, tools, and other unique pseudo-technological resources in possession of the organization have been classified as SCP-1000-001 through SCP-1000-███. These resources have been made use of by the Foundation in multiple instances; for a full list, see Document 1000-3534-Y (Level 3 clearance required). Access to surviving ex-members of the Children of the Sun is restricted to personnel with clearance level 4/1000 unless given direct authorization for contact by Director Jones.

Further information is available to personnel with clearance level 3/1000 or above. Personnel with clearance level 3/1000 or above are required to read Document Alpha-1596-1000.

Addendum 1000-466-X: Update to Special Containment Procedures: As of ■/■/■■■, SCP-1000's Special Containment Procedures no longer include Procedure 516-Lumina. [DATA EXPUNGED] indicates that SCP-1000 may be developing a resistance to the sonic element [DATA EXPUNGED] will not develop further, so that Procedure 516-Lumina can still be used in emergency situations. Investigation into alternate means of reliably keeping SCP-1000 away from human population centers is underway. Whether SCP-1000 resistance to Procedure 516-Lumina was calculated (and as such may be a sign of SCP-1000 [REDACTED]) or coincidental (by chance of natural species variation) is not known at this time.

== **LEVEL 3 CLEARANCE REQUIRED** ==

Document Alpha-1596-1000: Missive from Director Jones

You've probably heard the rumors before now. Everyone without the clearance level to know better wants to get their dig in. "Did you hear Sasquatch is an SCP? Are we gonna capture and contain Batboy next?"

Yes. SCP-1000 is Bigfoot.

I'm sure you've snickered. Don't worry. Contrary to rumors, we don't actually assign you to "Keter duty" for finding something humorous.

You think Bigfoot is funny because we *want* you to think Bigfoot is funny. We've bankrolled Hollywood comedies and farcical documentaries, paid off men in gorilla suits, perpetrated hoaxes with bear prints and goat fur, bribed and brainwashed cartoonists to get especially silly depictions on children's television. Even the term "Bigfoot" comes from us, planted in the media in 1958, a term people would find even harder to take seriously than "Sasquatch".

Why? We'll get to that.

The information in the article that you've already read isn't entirely true. There are two direct lies, and plenty of lies of omission.

There is no such thing as the "anomalous pseudo-disease" referred to as SCP-1000-f1. SCP-1000 does not possess a magical death aura. In fact, SCP-1000 does not directly exhibit any anomalous effect whatsoever.

We also lied about SCP-1000's intelligence level. SCP-1000 aren't chimp-level smart. They're smarter - to be precise, they are exactly as smart as us.

That brings us to the lies of omission. That's what this letter is for. The lies came from me, so I figure the truth should come from me as well.

This is the story we got from the Children of the Sun who defected to us. It's a story we didn't believe - refused to believe, at first.

As you've already read, the apes we call SCP-1000 evolved alongside us. We walked in the daytime, they walked in the nighttime, our nocturnal siblings in the shadows.

But while we were still wandering hunter-gatherers, they… changed. Like we would, a few thousand years later. Tools. Weapons. Agriculture. Domesticated animals. Stable settlements. As humanity blinked in the Pleistocene sun, SCP-1000's population exploded across the night. They blanketed the planet in the tens of billions.

They made things that we still can't comprehend, even though we've thoroughly studied the surviving pieces. Organic technology. They made trees and birds of prey grow into fast-moving ships, herds of animals that became trains, bushes that became flying vehicles. From insects and pigeons they made things equivalent to cell phones, televisions, computers. Atomic bombs. The Children describe vast shining cities, stretching across glaciers and penetrating the deepest caverns, grown skyships of ivory and spider-silk, creatures tending them with hundreds of blinking eyes.

We were rare, like gorillas now, a few hundred thousand left at best. We avoided their settlements just like wild animals today avoid ours. SCP-1000 understood we were intelligent like them, but avoided us just as we avoided them, saw us as fairies, as gnomes, ascribed us supernatural powers, said we ate bad children while they slept in daylight. They fenced off our dwindling wild populations in conservatories, outlawed poaching but in the underground consumed our bones as aphrodisiacs.

Then their civilization fell. And we did it. By 'we' I don't mean the Foundation. By 'we', I mean humanity.

The story is muddy. Supposedly a trickster forest god showed humanity favor, showed us the master's tools and how to use them. Why we did it, we don't know. Perhaps they hunted us, perhaps we were simply afraid. Perhaps it was just that they fenced us in, unintentionally or not. We simply don't know what the truth is. Somehow we acquired SCP-1000's own technology, and with it, we instigated an SK-class dominance shift in which humanity became the dominant species of Earth.

We wiped out 70% of SCP-1000's population in a single day. The Day of Flowers, the Children called it. Supposedly every flower bloomed that day, while our enemies died in their sleep. Then we hunted the rest down. But we went further than just killing them. With a few of the more twisted of SCP-1000's devices, we drove the survivors mad, even those hiding beyond our reach. We trapped them in their own minds, blocking higher functions and leaving their bodies to fend for themselves like any ordinary ape. We slaughtered their living machines and burned their vast shining cities with SCP-1000's bioweapons that reduced everything to slurry and dust that washed or blew away in spring rain and wind.

We left no traces. Not even our own memory. We turned one of the weapons on ourselves, wiped out any knowledge of SCP-1000 and the greatest civilization the planet had ever seen. Only a few humans protected themselves from the effect, kept the forbidden knowledge, just in case. The rest of us went back to being hunter-gatherers, none the wiser.

Which brings us to today. You're going to read all about this in the level 3 documentation, but I'll give you the short version here: SCP-1000 are somehow regaining their forgotten intelligence and knowledge. Maybe they never truly lost it. We don't know.

This is why the ever-increasing number of "Bigfoot sightings" is so worrying. Why the attempts at contact, however indecipherable, are even more worrying.

Yes. SCP-1000 *are* just like us. That's what makes them so dangerous. We wiped them from history and memory. We dissolved their civilization and we slaughtered most of their species. Just ask yourselves: If they got the chance, what more would they do to us?

Addendum 1000-056-D: Instances of SCP-1000 have tried to make contact with Foundation personnel on multiple occasions. Most of these attempts at contact have [DATA EXPUNGED] untranslated, though recent attempts show that some instances of SCP-1000 are capable of communicating in English.

Addendum 1000-104-Y: Certain acquired documents contain extensive references to SCP-1000. Relevant is that the documents appear to be composed by entities associated directly with the location known as the Wanderer's Library. Context or significance of document details not yet clarified.

Addendum 1000-276-A: Numerous anomalous objects with a known connection to SCP-1000 [DATA EXPUNGED] prior cyclical iterations. As one example, SCP-2273 may not have a point of origin in a parallel timeline, but instead a prior "iteration". SCP-2932, SCP-2511, and other sources of living cultural insight into SCP-1000 (or a variation) all present "consistent inconsistencies" which may be used to create a fuller picture of the nature of these "iterations", though conclusions are uncertain.

Addendum 1000-276-Q: Special report [DATA EXPUNGED] This unnumbered "black box" anomalous item anchored underneath the structure is likely the most significant anomalous object known to have been utilized. Central to understanding SCP-1000's anomalous capabilities, including capabilities not developed directly, but accessed from prior [DATA EXPUNGED] modern-day relevance to the Foundation and to society at large in a scenario of general containment failure.

Log 1000-ad065-x1: The following is a rough translation of recent SCP-1000 attempt at communication with Foundation personnel on ■/■/■ (see attached documentation).

we forgive you;
given choice for now, not forever;
let us back in

SCP-3844

Uploader Note: The following documentation is the earliest Foundation record of SCP-3844. However, this was originally drafted before the Foundation formalized the process of describing containment procedures and anomalies. It is archived here solely for posterity.

Correspondence From The Dolomite Mountains Regarding Anomalous Activity

21st of April, 1906

Dear Fredrick,

A dragon. There was a dragon in the mountains. And it looked just like we'd imagined.

Galviston and I had to follow our guide for about six hours before we first saw the beast. It soared over one peak, let out a low roar that loosened snow from the mountainside, and then dived out of sight. Its wings blocked out the sun like a cloud passing over head. I wish the whole lab could have seen it.

It took us another two hours to reach the dragon's cavern. It was a massive cave, filled with gems and goblets and other such valuables. We never reached the end of that cave, but judging from the echoes our footfalls made, we would've needed rations to make it there.

We gave up our search for the dragon for the day, thinking it was still flying about, and started our return trek to the outside. And then, just as we summited the last hill of treasure, we heard that roar. We froze, unsure if the noise came from our front or our back. The tension only faded after it spoke.

It welcomed us as guests.

The dragon motioned for us to come closer as it ambled in front of the maw of the cave. It had an accent like yours! Except lower and more gravelly. It took Galviston and I a few moments to come to our senses, and our guide a few more.

The beast was quite the gentlemen if I do say so. It changed its form to resemble a young man to make us feel more relaxed. I held a lengthy discussion with it while Galviston took notes. It was surprisingly well-versed in modern-day affairs. When I introduced ourselves as men of science, it called us "a new age of knights".

But do not fret, I did my duty. I'm surprised it worked, given our extreme lack of resources. I negotiated reasonable terms to keep the dragon contained within the Dolomites. I've transcribed the exact operating procedure below, but it agreed in writing. I can only hope it doesn't double cross us. But until then, those Italian officials should be content with our work, even if we've never handled an anomaly this massive before.

I will return once I've met with the Italians again to organize the whole affair. Next time Fredrick, you'll come with us. You and George and the whole lab! Words cannot do this majestic beast justice. I'll bring some gin so we can drink together one day.

Sincerely, Lester

Here are the negotiation terms:

The dragon known as Tharnock (henceforth "The Anomaly") has agreed to:

- Limit expeditions from its abode to one (1) time per day.

- Expeditions will remain within the confines of the Dolomite Mountains, and will maintain a low elevation.

- Refrain from vocalizing during expeditions.

In return, the Anomaly Investigation Foundation (henceforth "The Foundation") has agreed to:

- Recruit one (1) ambassador to interact with The Anomaly once per week.

- Punish any attempts to steal valuables from The Anomaly.

To maintain the secrecy of The Anomaly, the Nation of Italy (henceforth "The State") will:

- Discourage civilians from entering the Dolomite Mountains.

- Discredit any accounts of The Anomaly.

NOTICE FROM THE RECORDS AND INFORMATION SECURITY ADMINISTRATION

You are currently viewing an out of date version of this file that has been preserved for posterity. Please note that information presented herein may be misleading or incorrect.

Item #: SCP-3844
Object Class: Euclid

Special Containment Procedures: While proper facilities are under construction, SCP-3844 is to be contained at its dwelling within the Dolomite Mountains. A 100m x 100m perimeter is to be regularly patrolled by Foundation personnel to ensure no civilians come into contact with SCP-3844.

Anti-aircraft artillery is to be positioned around SCP-3844's dwelling. Artillery is to fire at any airborne entities over the containment perimeter. Any evidence of the existence of SCP-3844 is to be attributed to bombing runs.

Once a week, one D-Class is to be sent to interact with SCP-3844. Stealing items from SCP-3844 is prohibited.

Description: SCP-3844 is a winged reptile, measuring 73.76m from tail to head with a wing span of 67.42m. It is estimated to mass 27,000kg. SCP-3844's scales are of a purple hue, except around the stomach where they are much lighter. SCP-3844 is capable of expelling fire at 3400°C from its mouth through an unknown method.

SCP-3844 is capable of speech in at least 14 languages, and has an extensive knowledge of world events. During interactions with personnel, SCP-3844 takes on the form of an adult male human, however SCP-3844 can mimic the appearance of any human.

SCP-3844 inhabits a cavern that contains a currently unquantified amount of valuable metals. SCP-3844 often burrows underneath these materials, where it presumably sleeps.

Addendum: The following is a transcript of an interview between Dr. Lester Fegmont and SCP-3844.

<Begin Log>

Fegmont: Good evening.

SCP-3844: Lester! It's been decades, I believe. Although I guess you never specified a time for your return visit. Or circumstances.

Fegmont: I'm sorry about the err… updates, but war time calls for extreme measures.

SCP-3844: Ah, so the new-age knights still fight old-time battles.

Fegmont: I wouldn't say that we fight really. We just make sure the battles don't expose things people aren't supposed to see.

SCP-3844: Like me?

Fegmont: Yes, like you. But trust me, there are much, much worse things.

SCP-3844: I see. Did you at least bring the gin this time?

Fegmont: *[smiles]* I might run the show around here, but I still can't drink on the job.

SCP-3844: *[laughs]* Next time, then.

Fegmont: Of course.

SCP-3844: And will I ever be allowed to fly again?

Fegmont: Hopefully. But not before the war ends.

SCP-3844: The war is your whole world, isn't it?

Fegmont: Not so much. Governments just pay us to keep anomalies out of the hands of the other side. Can't imagine what would happen if people got ahold of anomalous rifles or—

SCP-3844: Dragons.

Fegmont: Yes, dragons.

Silence.

SCP-3844: Do you still perform research like you used to? I remember how you spoke of the lab.

Fegmont: We do. We do. One day, this war will end, but others of uh… your type show no signs of slowing down.

SCP-3844: Sharpening your swords.

Fegmont: I guess that's the apt analogy.

SCP-3844: And your fellow men eye me the same way knights did too. Like a prize.

Fegmont: They're just taking the measurements I should've made when we first met. I'll come back when we discover new things to evaluate.

SCP-3844: And at the end of the war, right?

Fegmont: And at the end of the war.

SCP-3844: I do hope I can trust you to uphold that.

Fegmont: Of course you can. But until then, do you have any further questions? I believe all of mine have been answered.

SCP-3844: Don't worry about me when there are larger issues at hand. You have a war to fight after all.

<**End Log**>

NOTICE FROM THE RECORDS AND INFORMATION SECURITY ADMINISTRATION

You are currently viewing an out of date version of this file that has been preserved for posterity. Please note that information presented herein may be misleading or incorrect.

Item #: SCP-3844
Object Class: Euclid

Special Containment Procedures: While proper facilities are under construction SCP-3844 is to be contained at its dwelling within the Dolomite Mountains. A 100m x 100m perimeter is to be regularly patrolled by Foundation personnel to ensure no civilians come into contact with SCP-3844. Anti-aircraft artillery is to be positioned around SCP-3844's dwelling. Artillery is to fire at any airborne entities over the containment perimeter. Any evidence of the existence of SCP-3844 is to be attributed to bombing runs. Artillery is only to be used in the event of a full scale containment breach.

Once a week, one D-Class member of the SCP-3844 project is to be sent to interact with SCP-3844, and take temperature and radiation measurements. A team of researchers are to take size measurements, perform IQ tests, and determine the maximum temperature of fire SCP-3844 can expel once per month. Personnel caught stealing items from SCP-3844 are to be disciplined accordingly.

SCP-3844 is to be provided with the following reading material as part of its monthly measurements:

- Time Magazine
- Science Magazine
- Nature Magazine
- Communications of the ACM

Description: SCP-3844 is a winged reptile, measuring ~~73.76m~~ 50.22m from tail to head, and with a wing span of ~~67.42m~~ 42.78m[1]. It is estimated to mass ~~27,000kg~~ 18,000kg. SCP-3844's scales are of a purple blue hue, except around the stomach where they are much lighter. SCP-3844 is capable of expelling fire at 3400°C from its mouth through an unknown method forcefully expelling a methane vapor from its mouth (achieving temperatures as high as 1950°C), and igniting it through unknown means.

SCP-3844 is capable of speech in at least ~~14~~ 7 languages, and has an ~~extensive~~ moderate knowledge of world events. During direct interactions with personnel, SCP-3844 takes the form of an adult male, however SCP-3844 claims it can mimic the appearance of any human.

SCP-3844 inhabits an immense cavern that contains a ~~currently unquantified amount of valuable metals~~ 2.69×10^6 kg of valuable metals (approximately 2.6 billion US dollars). SCP-3844 often burrows underneath these materials, where it presumably sleeps.

In conversation, SCP-3844 has confirmed that it is the inspiration behind a number of european myths involving dragons. It also claims to be the model for the Welsh flag[2].

Addendum: The following is a transcript of an interview between Dr. Lester Fegmont O5-2 and SCP-3844.

\<**Begin Log**\>

SCP-3844: I see you've finally returned. A few years late, but I guess that's only to be expected.

O5-2: Yes, I guess I am a little late. Sorry about that.

SCP-3844: Don't worry about it. You're obviously busy, and in the meantime, I've had all manner of new reading material. How long had you known about the nature of light?

O5-2: *[smiles]* Decades at least.

SCP-3844: And the inner workings of our smallest building block?

O5-2: We cracked open the atom during the war.

SCP-3844: Before long you might have an explanation for my kind!

O5-2: Well, you'd be surprised how far science can get you. My division has discovered that some things aren't even anomalous in the first place.

SCP-3844: So, has science finally found a way to let me stretch my wings?

O5-2: Unfortunately, due to certain advances in radar, we can't risk you leaving the cavern. However, I've asked others to devise a way to possibly… expand your home.

SCP-3844: Oh have you? I'm looking forward to this now.

O5-2: I do have to be on my way. Hopefully I will see you again.

SCP-3844: I hope so as well.

\<**End Log**\>

Item #: SCP-3844

Object Class: ~~Euclid~~ Neutralized

Special Containment Procedures: The remains of SCP-3844 are to be kept in a standard containment locker for non-anomalous materials. The former location of SCP-3844's dwelling is to be inspected once every 72 hours for possible anomalous activity.

Description: SCP-3844 ~~is~~ was a winged reptile, measuring ~~50.22m~~ 10.30m from tail to head, and with a wing span of ~~42.78m~~ 8.33m[1]. It ~~is~~ was estimated to weigh ~~18,000kg~~ 235kg. SCP-3844's scales ~~are were~~ of a pale blue hue, except around the stomach where they ~~are much lighter~~ were completely white. SCP-3844 ~~is~~ was capable of forcefully expelling a methane vapor from its mouth (achieving temperatures as high as 1950°C), and igniting it through unknown means through an instantaneous application of thaumaturgical incantation #043.

SCP-3844 ~~is~~ was capable of speech in ~~7~~ at most 2 languages, and has ~~moderate~~ had little knowledge of world events. During interactions with personnel, SCP-3844 ~~takes~~ took the form of an adult male, however SCP-3844 claims it can mimic the appearance of any human[2].

SCP-3844 ~~inhabits~~ inhabited an immense cavern that ~~contains~~ contained approximately 5.22×10^4kg of valuable metals (approximately ~~2.6 billion~~ 13.4 million US 1984 dollars). SCP-3844 often ~~burrows~~ burrowed underneath these materials, where it presumably sleeps.

In conversation, SCP-3844 ~~has~~ had confirmed that it is the inspiration behind a number of european myths involving dragons. It also ~~claims~~ claimed to be the model for the Welsh flag[3].

Addendum: The following is a transcript of the final interview between O5-2 and SCP-3844 before SCP-3844 attempted to breach containment.

<**Begin Log**>

SCP-3844: Why, hello. I'm a little surprised you showed up.

O5-2: You did ask to speak with the person in charge of your containment. I've been doing this since the beginning.

SCP-3844: It's not that I expected you to decline my request. I'm surprised you're still upright instead of laying down under the earth somewhere.

O5-2: I mean, it's nothing special. I tried to refuse, but the council insist they keep their figure head in pristine condition. It's just a bit of thaumaturgy and temporal technology.

SCP-3844: It's magic, is what it is.

O5-2: Everything is science when you examine it for long enough.

SCP-3844: That is more or less what I've learned over that past century or so. Which is really too bad.

O5-2: How so?

SCP-3844: Have you ever looked up at the stars as of late?

O5-2: Not really, no.

SCP-3844: Regardless, can you tell me what you would see?

O5-2: Stars?

SCP-3844: But what are stars?

O5-2: Balls of flaming gas. If you want me to be more specific I could list their chemical components.

SCP-3844: No, that's fine. I've read up on them myself. However, do you know what a duke once told me many, many years ago when I asked him the same thing?

O5-2: I believe he would've given a much less accurate answer.

SCP-3844: He said, "They're little lights from the heavens." His voice spoke with awe, much like yours when we first met.

O5-2: Are you grieving over the advancement of science? Upset that we can now understand you?

SCP-3844: No, I'm mourning the death of spectacles and miracles. I wish I could embrace science, but it takes away so much of what I enjoy about this world of ours. It appears I'm allergic to the stuff.

O5-2: Well, I don't have much I can do about that.

SCP-3844: I understand. It's fine. I think I'll finally have to break our agreement, although in fairness you did not exactly uphold your end.

O5-2: I can't just let you leave.

SCP-3844: I see no way for you to stop me. I really must be going. My wings have not felt the rush of air in a century, and I can hear my kin's beck and call.

O5-2: You seem quite confident.

SCP-3844: Confidence is all I have left. I don't want to believe that the world doesn't need its whimsy anymore.

<End Log>

SCP-3844 was terminated by the anti-aircraft artillery stationed around its dwelling. However, inspection of SCP-3844's projected trajectory uncovered the remains of a non-anomalous *Draco volans*[4].

Additionally, the location of SCP-3844 no longer contained a large cavern, but instead a small hole, approximately 1m deep, and 2m in diameter.

NOTICE FROM THE RECORDS AND INFORMATION SECURITY ADMINISTRATION

The following is a provisional document, and may contain incorrect or incomplete information. This document is to be updated as investigation progresses.

Item #: SCP-3844
Object Class: Keter (pending review)

Special Containment Procedures: O5-2 has been assigned to oversee the investigation of SCP-3844 and the development of appropriate long-term containment procedures. Until this time, O5-2 will act as necessary to ensure the Foundation's objectives are met in regards to the anomaly.

Description: SCP-3844 is the collective designation for numerous, large, winged lizards located within the Himalayans, Rockies, Appalachians, Andes and Dolomites.

Uploader's Note: Dragons. There are still dragons in the mountains.

SCP-435

Item #: SCP-435

Object Class: Keter

Special Containment Procedures: SCP-435-1 is to be kept in a secure warehousing facility that constantly provides SCP-435-1 a minimum of 1000 lux illumination. Illumination must be provided by redundant lamps operating from at least three parallel and independent power supplies providing generator and battery backups. Tests for integrity of the lighting system shall be conducted on a daily basis. In addition, two mobile units capable of transporting SCP-435-1 shall remain on standby in the event of Contingency 435-XK-Alpha. No other special protective procedures are required to examine or test SCP-435-1, but research may only be conducted on SCP-435-1 with written O5 approval.

At ground level, a secure perimeter is to be kept for 50 km around SCP-435-2. A no-fly zone of 125 km is to be maintained in the airspace surrounding SCP-435-2. At least two Foundation aircraft and one mobile ground station are to monitor the size and position of SCP-435-2 at all times. Should monitoring detect any growth of SCP-435-2, or any motion of SCP-435-2 relative to SCP-435-1 for a period in excess of 90 seconds, observation teams are to initiate Contingency 435-XK-Alpha. No personnel are to approach within 100 meters of SCP-435-2, and Foundation security teams are authorized to take any action to prevent such contact. No research or testing is authorized on SCP-435-2 without explicit O5 direction.

Description: SCP-435-1 is a type III iron meteorite weighing approximately ██,███ kg, showing significant weathering. Spectroscopic and chemical analysis shows a composition over 99% iron, which at normal densities can only account for ██% of the measured weight. Age is indeterminate, but analysis of weathering suggests it has been exposed to atmosphere for at least ██,███ years.

SCP-435-2 is an irregularly shaped object that currently has approximate dimensions of 15 m x 12 m x 48 m. SCP-435-2 appears somewhat blurred in the visible spectrum, but computer-enhanced imagery in various spectra has shown a complex structure showing a three-fold symmetry along the longitudinal axis. Extending from the axis are long tube-like structures that share characteristics both with biological organisms (in particular, cephalopods of the order Teuthida) and with mathematical models of higher-order fractals. These structures show undulating movements even when SCP-435-2 is stationary. SCP-435-2 does not appear to have mass or inertia, and appears only to be visible due to refraction of light passing through it, and because of [DATA EXPUNGED] resulting in Cherenkov radiation of varying intensity. Any physical object with mass that comes in contact with SCP-435-2 will suffer an instantaneous change in velocity and direction away from SCP-435-2 without any loss in energy. This is apparently caused by being reflected through a higher-order spatial dimension. If the affected mass is in a solid phase, this reflection will cause a change in topology that can result in either an inversion (turning inside out), a reflection (mirroring of all or part of physical structure), or a [DATA EXPUNGED] and high levels of gamma radiation.

Because of these characteristics, it is currently impossible to directly affect SCP-435-2 with any means currently at the Foundation's disposal. However, it can be moved indirectly by moving SCP-435-1. SCP-435-2 maintains a fixed position relative to SCP-435-1 as long as SCP-435-1 is sufficiently illuminated. (SCP-435-2's current position is ███ km northwest of SCP 435-1 on a vector ██° above the horizon; about ████ m above sea-level.) Movements of SCP-435-1 have caused SCP-435-2 to move a proportional amount, maintaining a fixed distance and bearing.

If SCP-435-1 ceases to be sufficiently illuminated for a period of time exceeding 8.3 μs, the behavior of SCP-435-2 will change. SCP-435-2 will enter an active state and begin random erratic movements orbiting the location of SCP-435-1. Average distance from SCP-435-1 will increase, and the apparent volume of SCP-435-2 will also increase. The rate of increase in both distance and size appears to undergo a geometric progression over time, and neither has been observed to decrease. This behavior will cease once SCP-435-1 is again sufficiently illuminated, at which point SCP-435-2 will cease motion at whatever location it is at that moment, and remain there fixed in relation to SCP-435-1. The threshold for this effect currently appears to be between 500 and 650 lux, and it appears that this threshold may increase by approximately ██% whenever SCP-435-2 enters an active state.

Because of SCP-435-2's interaction with normal matter, an active state is considered extremely dangerous. Passing through large volumes of air at speeds in excess of 500 m/s dramatically increases levels of radiation, and if SCP-435-2 intersects water or any land mass [DATA EXPUNGED]. Any active state lasting longer than 90 seconds constitutes a potential XK-class end-of-the-world scenario and requires the initiation of Contingency 435-XK-Alpha.

Addendum 1: Recovery Notes SCP-435

[REDACTED] SCP-435-2 in active state [REDACTED] March 195█

SCP-435-1 was recovered in 195█ at ████ ████, ████ ████. While surveying sites for testing a ████ ██, the US Army Corps of Engineers were directed to evacuate the native population from ██, a small island 85 km from the proposed test site. They met heavy resistance from the local population. After evacuating the island by force, they discovered SCP-435-1 in a clearing surrounded by several dozen burning torches. At this time SCP-435-2 was not in an observable location, and the US authorities had no indication of any anomalies. A survey crew was left behind, and according to subsequent interviews, when half the torches burned out [DATA EXPUNGED] as a result of SCP-435-2 moving through [DATA EXPUNGED] before illumination restored to SCP-435-1. Foundation then took custody of SCP-435 and the US government provided a cover story code name ████ ██, explaining that [REDACTED] was the result of a [REDACTED] having a higher yield than expected.

Addendum 2: Interview with one of the Village Elders evacuated from ██ by US Army Corps of Engineers in February 195█.

Interviewed: ████, Male 75 years of age, former resident of ██, ████ ██, recovery site for SCP-435-1

Interviewer: Dr. Richards

Foreword: Interview is part of background research on the history of SCP-435 prior to Foundation custody.

<Begin Log, 1/12/196█ 1430>

Dr. Richards: What do you know about SCP-435-1?

██: The sky rock?

Dr. Richards: Yes, the "sky rock."

██: There is a story to it.

Dr. Richards: Tell it to us.

██: Long ago, when the world was only water and sky, there were two brothers, "He-Who-Made-Light" and "He-Who-Made-Dark." Like all brothers they fought. One time the light brother insulted the work of the dark brother. The dark one, he does not like this, and begins to destroy all the light in the world. "He-Who-Made-Light" cannot let this be so he shoves his brother into a hole that goes outside light and dark, and plugs the hole with a rock. Because "He-Who-Made-Dark" can only see in the dark, "He-Who-Made-Light" puts the rock in a sling and throws it around the sun so it will always stay lit and the dark one will never see how to find his way out.

Dr. Richards: That rock is SCP-435-1?

██: That is your name for the sky rock.

Dr. Richards: Yes it is. How did it end up [REDACTED]

██████████: Long after the brothers fought, the dark one's rock fell from the sky. It fell so hard that it broke the Earth and raised the land and killed the first people who lived only in the sea. On the Earth, the sun lit it only half the time, so when darkness came, "He-Who-Made-Dark" could see to find his way. Even so, he had been lost outside the world for many many years, so each night he only came a little closer. And each night the rocks shook and bled fire at his approach. The Earth did not like this, so she made the second people to watch over the sky rock, and keep it lit so that the dark one cannot find his way home. [pauses] I think you may be the third people.

Dr. Richards: So do you have any measure of how long you were keeping it lit?

██████████: Since before [DATA EXPUNGED] *Note: geological formations in the area suggest that if this is true then habitation of* ██████ *predates known human populations in the area by nearly ten-thousand years.*

Dr. Richards: [Shows ██████████ a photo of SCP-435-2] Do you know what this is?

██████████: Y-yes.

Dr. Richards: Is it "He-Who-Made-Dark"?

██████████: No. [pauses] It is his shadow.

\<End Log\>

Closing Statement: *The non-material nature of SCP-435-2 lends credence to the hypothesis that it is a projected effect from an unknown extra-dimensional entity somehow bound to SCP-435-1. While dumping the rock into SCP-██ and making it another universe's problem is tempting, it seems possible that the actual effect would be to only transport SCP-435-1 without transporting the entity it appears to contain, releasing "He-Who-Made-Dark" into the material universe. Therefore Contingency 435-XK-Alpha is only a last resort.* — O5-█

SCP-2264

Item #: SCP-2264

Object Class: Safe

Martin Tower, Tower of London.

Special Containment Procedures: Due to the unavoidably public nature of the building housing SCP-2264-A, security measures are to focus on preventing civilian access to the anomaly's entrance. The Foundation is to cooperate with the government of the United Kingdom in concealing the existence of SCP-2264-A. A hidden passage to SCP-2264-A has been constructed and remains its only means of access. The original entrance to the room where SCP-2264-A is located has been walled over, ensuring that only authorized personnel have access to SCP-2264-A. Operatives are to be reassigned and replaced monthly due to the threat of psychological addiction to SCP-2264-B.

Description: SCP-2264-A is a door composed of iron located within a hidden chamber beneath Martin Tower, a part of the Tower of London.[1] The gateway cannot be unlocked through traditional means, requiring a highly ritualized process. Attached to SCP-2264-A is a complex apparatus composed of alchemical tools such as alembics, retorts, and a crucible.

Henry Percy, 9th Earl of Northumberland.

Based on journals found within the hidden chamber, SCP-2264-A[2] is presumably the creation of Henry Percy (27 April 1564 - 5 November 1632), 9th Earl of Northumberland, an English aristocrat, alchemist, and long-term prisoner within the Tower of London. Despite his incarcerated status, the Earl maintained a degree of influence, said to enjoy a comfortable lifestyle and allowed access to books and research material. He was known as The Wizard Earl due to his extensive library and interests in the scientific and occult.

It is considered possible that others within Percy's circle of associates were involved in the creation of SCP-2264-A, including John Dee, famed alchemist and court astrologer of Queen Elizabeth. The School of Night,[3] of which Henry Percy was supposedly member to, may have also had involvement.

Journal of Henry Percy, The Wizard Earl:

Nigredo:
we will confront the dark night of the soul - the [pineal gland] will be freshly extract'd. fire evokes the shadow within.

Albedo:
wash aroint the impurities - rain cleanses all sin and prepares the soul f'r Elysium. divide, not as dictat'd by the rigors of harmony, but rather into two opposing principles to be later coagulat'd to form a unity of opposites.

Citrinitas:
victory coincides with the yellowing of the lunar consciousness. the white
surrenders to dawn; the travelling lamp slays the moon.

Rubedo:
red alludes; instead, surrender upon the apparatus a sanguine sacrifice.

A Foundation alchemist was consulted. The instructions are roughly comparable
with the *magnum opus*; a four-part process employed in the creation of the
mythical philosopher's stone. Replication of this procedure required
[REDACTED].[4]

Through still undetermined means, a mechanism within SCP-2264-A responds to
the completed solution, causing it to unlock and open - allowing access to
SCP-2264-B.

SCP-2264-B is an extradimensional city which does not correspond to any known
location, earthly or otherwise. Objects that originate from within SCP-2264-B
will dematerialize if brought through SCP-2264-A. Such objects have been
later found returned to the site of their initial removal.

Those who enter SCP-2264-B report having all personal belongings removed and
their clothes replaced. Manifested outfits are said to resemble those worn at
masquerade balls, most especially those associated with the Carnival of
Venice, and will dematerialize upon exit of SCP-2264-B. Masks cannot be
removed while inside SCP-2264-B but the rest of the attire can be discarded
if one chooses to do so. The majority of SCP-2264-B inhabitants are dressed
and adorned in a similar fashion; agents have reported a somewhat organic
quality to their costumes, frequently describing it as "chitinous". The most
common inhabitants of SCP-2264-B are roughly humanoid and have since have
been classified as SCP-2264-1.

The sky has been described as yellow and containing an indeterminate number
of black stars, corresponding with no known or even hypothesized
constellations. Buildings are shaped in such a manner as to suggest them
being carved from a single seamless material. Black, white, yellow, and red
are the only colors to reportedly occur within SCP-2264-B. Architecture is
non-euclidean and the normal laws of gravity do not apply,[5] thus inhabitants
can be observed as climbing a stairway upside-down, but based on their own
gravity source, they are climbing normally.

The city has been described as having the odor of "dried flowers with a hint
of mold", or a scent "not unlike that of old books". The actual size of the
city has been difficult to measure but it appears to be located on an island,
surrounded by a black ocean, the composition of the liquid is unknown but
described as appearing more viscous than water.

Operatives have reported a hypnagogic malaise while exploring SCP-2264-B,
with difficulty estimating time and space. Although SCP-2264-B is a tangible
location and not considered to be an actual dream, those who had a history of
lucid dreaming have shown far greater self-control and attention to detail
than those who did not. Operatives are to be reassigned and replaced monthly

due to the threat of psychological addiction to SCP-2264-B. Initial efforts at exploration resulted in eight AWOL operatives with those that returned having difficulty describing what they had observed in a coherent and/or detailed manner.

The almost hypnagogic nature of SCP-2264-B has led many to observe it as a dream or hallucination, failing to fully recognize its inherent verisimilitude. A lucid dreamer and an experienced user of hallucinogenics, I (Dr. Calixto Narváez), was well chosen for this mission. My comrades quickly surrendered to the anomaly, engaging in the decadent pleasures of the city; most especially within the palace.

Tempting as it was, I did not join the others in their rapturous orgy. I would suggest interviewing those that previously entered SCP-2264-B again; it is unlikely they've gone into all the details. When allowed a chance to directly control a dream, so many claim they would fly or visit the stars; those people are liars. Most choose to surrender to the ecstatic delirium of sexual pleasure.

Again, this is not a dream, but I am able to understand why most are unable to perceive the difference. I am reminded of the legend of the Hassassins, how their leader supposedly drugged and led his recruits into his castle; within was a pleasure garden that rivaled any imagined paradise - the individuals truly believed they were offered a taste of the divine. SCP-2264-B works in a somewhat similar way but I do not believe that is the reason for its splendor. I doubt it is intended to be a trap. It is simply a city (although certainly a majestic city unlike anything I had ever before encountered) but one that happens to exist outside baseline reality and does not entirely conform to the physical rules we are used to.

I have made significant discoveries while exploring SCP-2264-B:

1. Universal translation of language - while most of the agents perceive the inhabitants as speaking English, I heard them in my native tongue of Spanish. Even those of my team, when communicating with me directly, appeared to have been speaking Spanish while within the anomaly. I have discovered that this is also applied to written language but not quite as accurately.

Written words initially appear as alien shapes; most of the symbols having a somewhat spiral-like pattern. If one continues to directly observe the symbols, they will begin to blur and alter until some level of translation has manifested. However, there do appear to be limitations and it seems that some words native to SCP-2264-B have no equivalent in any human language. The words appear to move on paper and prolonged exposure can easily result in nausea and headache.

2. The true name of SCP-2264-B is Alagadda, a city-state said to border the Nevermeant.[6] I was able to gather much of this information from the Wandsman of Kul-Manas, a scholar and foreigner like myself. They wore a beaked mask and exquisite robes cloaked their hunchbacked form; their hands were scaly (more avian than reptilian) with black talons. They unfurled a scroll before

me, said it was a map of the multiverse - layer after layer of endless spirals - I sense an oncoming migraine just thinking about it now.

Regardless, I was pleased to meet a fellow intellectual within. I asked them about the nature of their research. "What is the nature of all that is?" they asked, I assumed rhetorically. "Just for a start," they noted.

3. There is a specific power structure within SCP-2264-B, involving entities that, based on description, could easily be considered some of the more dangerous reality benders known to the Foundation. The Wandsman of Kul-Manas warned of individuals that should not even be approached, less we draw undesirable attention to our reality.

There are (or were) four Masked Lords who directly oversee SCP-2264-B:

The Black Lord, Wearer of the Anguished Mask
The White Lord, Wearer of the Diligent Mask
The Yellow Lord, Wearer of the Odious Mask
The Red Lord, Wearer of the Mirthful Mask

They were said to be the chief advisors to the King of Alagadda. They continued to warn that I not be fooled by their names; each just as terrible as the other. I have seen the Masked Lords, always at a distance, all except the Wearer of the Anguished Mask. I was informed that the Black Lord was the victim of a political struggle some time ago (the reason never known, if reason existed at all) and cast into some dreadful dimensional backwater. It would only be a matter of time before they returned.

The insidious glamour of the city-state disguises a dreadful truth, one the Wandsman had difficulty expressing in words. They stated that most outsiders came to this place to seek a boon from the King. They refused to speak anymore of this entity and suggested I avoid the Ambassador of Alagadda as well, before politely taking their leave of me.

I decided it time to report back, gathered the others (pulling a few from the writhing mound of masked transdimensional entities); the first door we entered was the one to return us to baseline reality. I suspect that SCP-2264-B is a dimensional nexus, connected to countless worlds across the multiverse. Every door used within SCP-2264-B has connected directly to SCP-2264-A. If there are other gateways like SCP-2264-A, I suspect them to be currently sealed.

Dr. Calixto Narváez was commended for his initiative. A psychological evaluation has determined it safe for him to reenter in the near future, although it has been requested that he use a more professional tone with regards to his reports. Future operatives will be screened for higher than normal levels of activity in the parietal lobes while in a state of altered consciousness (sleep or otherwise).

The "Wandsman of Kul-Manas" has since been classified as SCP-2264-2 and is considered an invaluable source of information. The "Masked Lords of Alagadda" have been classified as SCP-2264-3.

I believe SCP-2264-2 is the only entity we might truly trust in Alagadda and sought them immediately. The city contains thousands, if not millions, but SCP-2264-2 stands out and appears to have a strictly scholarly interest in SCP-2264-B - most especially the palace library.

The collection was impressive and could have been infinite in size for all I knew (there was no visible end to the room, the corridor stretching long into the horizon). I wandered the seemingly endless hall, Agent Cromwell and Dr. Yu at my side, in search of SCP-2264-2. I scanned through a few grimoires and scrolls, the alien symbols failing to translate (leading me to suspect that no earthly translation was possible).

In time we found SCP-2264-2, affable as before and expressing concern about our well-being. I asked that they elaborate and I write their response as best as my memory allows:

"The Ambassador of Alagadda will soon return from Adytum and only the mad shall remain. I suggest you leave posthaste, for I intend the same."

I thanked them for their warning and declared that we would not linger for long. I asked them about Adytum. They replied:

"A terrible city, filled with equally terrible people. It is said that the Grand Karcist of Adytum serves the designs of an elder being, a horror thought to rival even the Hanged King of Alagadda. Craw! (SCP-2264-2 made a sound not unlike a crow) I should not speak of them. Not here."

I asked about who they were (SCP-2264-2), wanting to know more about them. They replied:

"I am the Wandsman of Kul-Manas. A scholar, as you undoubtedly know. I am a walker of the astral plane, a sailor of the celestial sea, and a spelunker of the planar deep."

SCP-2264-2 noted something about our "aura"; declaring it rare across the multiverse but admitted to having encountered similar during previous visits to SCP-2264-B. They said something along the lines of:

"The Deathless Merchant of London; driven by greed and black ambition. There was another; a stranger in a strange land. It appeared as though they did not know where they were, smelling of fear. I cannot imagine how one might accidentally stumble upon Alagadda, I did not believe such a thing was possible. They vanished soon after yet I never witnessed them leave. Simply gone in a blink."

They would continue to reference the "Karcists" and "Clavigers" of Adytum, stating that they "reeked of decay and embryonic fluid". That was the extent of people encountered with a similar "aura" to our own; I suspect SCP-2264-2 is able to sense a person's "dimensional neighborhood". SCP-2264-2 turned their head completely around (somewhat like an owl) and cawed, declaring:

"I sense the Ambassador of Alagadda has returned. I take my leave of this place and I suggest you do the same. Flee; do not delay. Perhaps I will pay your realm a visit in the future."

SCP-2264-2 exited the nearest door. The door refused to budge but I suspect it connected SCP-2264-2 to their native dimension. We exited the library, walking quickly (not wishing to bring too much attention upon ourselves by running). We found an unlocked door and returned home. We never saw the ambassador or their king, but I feel it best that we not seek them out.

Although not directly encountered, the Ambassador of Alagadda and the King of Alagadda have been respectively classified as SCP-2264-4 and SCP-2264-5.

The O5 Council voted 10 to 3 in support of sending Mobile Task Force Psi-9 ("Abyss Gazers") into SCP-2264-B. The goal of the operation was to locate SCP-2264-4 and SCP-2264-5 and calculate the level of threat they represented to humanity, Earth, and local dimensional space. Twelve agents, trained in hand-to-hand combat and Counter Occult Stratagems (COS), entered SCP-2264-A on ██/██/████ at 0800.

One agent returned alive; the rest are presumed dead or otherwise irretrievable.

Interviewed: Agent Alexander Papadopoulos

Interviewer: Dr. Laxmi Narang

Foreword: Agent Papadopoulos was found to be in critical condition upon their exit of SCP-2264, losing consciousness soon after. A physical examination revealed fractured bones throughout the entirety of their body and extensive internal bleeding. After three weeks of hospitalization, Agent Papadopoulos was deemed healthy enough for interview.

<Begin Log>

Dr. Laxmi Narang: I know it might be difficult but please tell me everything you remember.

Agent Alexander Papadopoulos: The city was remarkable. Command prepped us for it as best they could but words fail to do it justice. We all had the appearance of harlequins or something out of an old time masquerade. Wasn't exactly the same but close enough. Couldn't take the masks off, hard as we tried. We had a mission to complete but the details were quite vague.

Dr. Laxmi Narang: Vague?

Agent Alexander Papadopoulos: Find SCP-2264-4 and -5; get an estimate on their threat level. We knew they were important to SCP-2264 but we had no idea what they looked like or how to locate them.

Dr. Laxmi Narang: Go on.

Agent Alexander Papadopoulos: Right. Well. We found the palace. Don't know how long it took. Time has no meaning in a place like that. The city is full of people, especially that palace, but it didn't feel like being in a busy city in our world. There was something different about it but I don't know how else to describe it. Layered? No, still not right. Not important I guess.

Things blurred a lot. Everything seemed to follow a sort of dream logic.

Dr. Laxmi Narang: Dream logic?

Agent Alexander Papadopoulos: Yeah. I mean. It wasn't a dream, I'm certain of that. And I have the scars to prove it. It was all real but have you ever noticed how dreams rush through the details? You end up one place but don't really recall how? It was like that. I remember the masquerade; the music and the dancing… oh, and the fucking. All with their masks on, of course. Seeing some of them "nude" was a shock. They aren't like us. Lets just say not everything was part of an elaborate costume. Their skin was like porcelain. I think those were the natives. You know, SCP-2264-1. But the more you stared, the less human everyone seemed; some had too many limbs, some had too few. They were like the monsters from an old fantasy comic I read as a kid. Crazy as this place was, I don't think we were ever seeing the whole truth. It's like a filter. The people look humanoid because we're human. Something from another world would see us more like them. But some… especially the natives… I got the feeling that behind those masks, beyond their illusions, was something inconceivable.

Sorry. Rambling. Head hurts trying to remember. [Becomes distracted] I can't move my arms or legs. What's wrong with them?

Dr. Laxmi Narang: The numbness is just a side effect of your medication. Please focus on my questions.

Agent Alexander Papadopoulos: Okay. If you say so. I remember having to pull Agent Maher away from some woman… I think it was a woman. Wasn't attacking him or anything. Quite the opposite, actually. Couldn't blame him. She had curves in all the right places - made it easy to ignore the tentacles.

So, the twelve of us stick together. Hard to not look like you're out for trouble with that many. Anyway, we wandered around the palace and it was like a labyrinth. I honestly wouldn't have been surprised if we stumbled into a minotaur or something. We spent most of the time descending the stairs, I think? I remember feeling like we were traveling deeper and deeper…

And then, somehow, just when we thought we had reached the bottom, we're back outside. It looked like we were in exactly the same spot as when we first entered SCP-2264-B. Hell, we could all see the palace in the distance.

But something was different. Everything was dark, drained of color. Like, we could see and all but it was a hazy gray twilight. The streets were empty and the buildings looked… ruined? Yeah. Was like the whole city was abandoned long ago. Desolate and silent; not a sound but our own footsteps.

We eventually entered this iteration of the palace. Everything was identical, at least the architecture.

That's when we heard the whispers. It spoke in a language I had never heard before. I could feel it slithering into my ear, eating its way to my brain…

We… [Begins to weep]

Dr. Laxmi Narang: Please continue.

Agent Alexander Papadopoulos: We destroyed ourselves.

Dr. Laxmi Narang: ...What?

Agent Alexander Papadopoulos: We had no choice. The Ambassador, it found us. It didn't have a face; no mouth, nose, or eyes. I thought it was wearing a skintight outfit and... high heels? That is what it looked like at first but no... that was its body. Its flesh was black. It stood tall, lithe and androgynous, and so.. so...

Dr. Laxmi Narang: Please, this information is important. Pace yourself. We can stop if...

Agent Alexander Papadopoulos: [Interrupting] It stood so damn proud. Just radiating arrogance. I couldn't understand a word it said and yet every syllable dripped with narcissistic venom. It brought a hand to where a mouth should have been... and it laughed and laughed... and then we destroyed ourselves for its amusement.

Our bones were shattered. Our flesh was torn open and our organs ruptured. We ruined ourselves in body and mind. All for that thing's amusement. And the whole time, I tried to scream, I tried to beg, but couldn't make a sound. "I'm so sorry", I tried to say, "I'm so sorry". My team. My friends. I remember how their eyes pleaded for mercy - and asked for forgiveness. You don't forget eyes like that.

In the end, I was the only one left alive - surrounded by the mutilated corpses that were once my team. I understand now. The Ambassador needed a witness, one to deliver its message. To tell you this... and... [Begins to hyperventilate]

Dr. Laxmi Narang: Please continue.

Agent Alexander Papadopoulos: I watched the ceiling move as it... as it dragged my broken body from room to room. Eventually we stopped and it lifted me up, held me up before the throne. There I saw the King. It was anchored in place, with hands and throat shackled tight, like... like a corpse in bondage. Its face was hidden beneath a black veil, or maybe it was a hood. I... I don't quite remember.

But I remember these horrid imps. They were caressing the King's twitching body, as if trying to comfort it. But others pulled the tethers even tighter. The King trembled and quivered and I saw pale tendrils slither in and out of its tattered robes. I looked on as the imps lifted the King's veil... [there is a change in tone, suggesting lucidity] I want to die. I can't live with what I've done. Please kill me. End this. I can't feel my legs. I can't feel my arms. Not like this. Not like this. Please, I'm begging you...

Dr. Laxmi Narang: You know I can't do that. Please tell me what you saw.

Agent Alexander Papadopoulos: [Said without emotion] A god shaped hole. The barren desolation of a fallen and failed creation. You see the light of long dead stars. Your existence is nothing but an echo of a dying god's screams. The unseen converges. Surrounds you. And it tightens like a noose.

<End Log>

Operations involving SCP-2264 are suspended until further notice. The agent's request for termination has been denied. Due to the considerable damage suffered, amputation of both arms and legs was deemed necessary, and subject is no longer able to perform most biological functions without the aid of life support systems. He is to be restrained for his own protection (despite his loss of limbs, suicide attempts have been made) and thoroughly interrogated for all possible information related to SCP-2264. Due to his contact with SCP-2264-4 and SCP-2264-5, he is to be quarantined and carefully observed for signs of anomaly. Agent Papadopoulos has refused food and water, requiring the use of a feeding tube.

Addendum: SCP-2264 was discovered accidentally during the refurbishment of Martin Tower in ██/██/████. The Foundation was contacted by representatives of the Crown due to the suspicion of a potentially anomalous artifact based on the writings found within, since attributed to Henry Percy, 9th Earl of Northumberland. Discovered among his notes was an unsent letter, intended to be received by Christopher Marlowe, famed poet and playwright. The letter is dated 30 May 1593, the day of Christopher Marlowe's unsolved murder.

Christopher Marlowe.

To my singular goode Friend, may this Missive reach thee ere 'tis too late.

'Twas thou who urg'd against my building of the Janus Gate. My Insult was cruell, having deem'd thee foolish and ignorant of the Sciences: I prithee forgive mine Arrogance.

'Twas thou who suffer'd the Evil to which I was blind. I show'd thee the Other Ordinary, and allow'd the secret Darknesse to coil around the Cinder of thy beautiful Heart. I was blind, but now I see.

I beseech thee to burn that accurs'd Play[7] and return it to Ashe. Thy Patron seeks to corrupt and defile: Whence He cometh, there are Things that simply should not be. The Ambassador shall exploit thee, as they did us. I have seal'd the Janus Gate so that only the Enlighten'd may enter. May they have the Wisdom to see what I coulde not, and the Power to slay the wretch'd King within.

Damn that Metropolis of Blood, that terrible Realm and its antient countless Crimes. Consign thy Play to the Fire, deny thy vile Patron, and aroint thee from this Madnesse. We would fain welcome thee backe into the Night.

Footnotes

1. Also known as Her Majesty's Royal Palace and Fortress.

2. Frequently referred to in notes as a Janus Gate. Janus is the Roman deity of beginnings and transitions, thereby associated with doors, doorways, gates, and passages.

3. A secret society interested in the study of science, philosophy, and religion; members were suspected of atheism, at the time not only considered blasphemous but an act of treason and anarchy.

4. To request this information, please contact the Department of Alchemical Studies.

5. This may be caused by multiple gravity wells within the city but this cannot be directly measured.

6. Meaning remains unknown.

7. "Seems likely the play being referred to here is SCP-701. Script should be investigated for more information on Alagadda." - Dr. Nkiru Diawara

SCP-2523

Item #: SCP-2523

Object Class: Euclid

Special Containment Procedures: Annually on August 15th, Mobile Task Force Omicron-13 ("Trick or Treat") is to be activated. MTF o-13 must begin a full Class W mnestic treatment regimen no later than August 20th. MTF o-13 will begin the Class W dosage ramp-down no earlier than November 7th, and will stand down no earlier than November 15th. Activation may be extended up to 90 days at the discretion of the SCP-2523 project lead (further extensions must be approved by both the reporting HR supervisor and the reporting medical officer).

Beginning on October 1st, MTF o-13 will conduct 24 hour observation of eight sites affected by SCP-2523 (designated SCP-2523-A through -H) which will include the easternmost and westernmost affected locations as well as one additional site chosen in each US timezone. On October 31st, one hour prior to local sunset, MTF o-13 will deploy a two-man contact team into each designated site. As each location enters the anomaly, teams will confirm positive contact and passphrase with each other prior to carrying out mission operations. Contact teams are to be relieved every eight hours for 24 hours. Ejected team members must be replaced immediately. All teams within the anomaly must confirm positive contact and passphrase during each relief or replacement.

Team members are to attempt to prevent non-monetary purchases by civilians, using low-profile social engineering techniques only. In the event that a civilian engages in non-monetary purchasing, they are to ascertain the civilian's identity and origin point, and advise the support team. Support teams are to immediately locate and detain any civilians who have made non-monetary purchases. Purchased items are to be confiscated for study. Detained persons are to be interviewed and then released following amnesticization. Ejected contact team personnel are to be immediately reclassified as Class E personnel, debriefed, and quarantined for 366 days at a location at least 50 km from any key Foundation assets. Survivors may return to duty pending approval by the reporting medical officer.

Currently, detention of SCP-2523-1 entities is not authorized. In the event that authorization is reinstated, entities are to be secured with restraints consisting of a minimum 75% iron by mass.

Description: SCP-2523 is a phenomenon affecting seasonal Halloween costuming and decoration stores in the US and Canada from sunset on October 31st to sunset on November 1st. It is restricted to stores which are entirely seasonal, and does not affect Halloween displays in more permanent businesses.

While the anomaly is active, the affected locations become spatially collocated, regardless of geographic separation. Store interiors will overlay where sufficiently similar (e.g., similar display shelving will become a single shelf unit without duplication of products); otherwise, the entire space expands as needed. Persons entering one location are able to physically interact with persons at all affected locations in real time, and return to their place of origin when exiting.[1]

The affected locations remain open for the full 24-hour period regardless of posted hours. At sunset, four to six entities (designated SCP-2523-1) will appear and relieve all employees. Entities are diminutive humanoids (estimated to be between 0.8 and 1.2 meters in height) with a variety of chimerical features from various vertebrates, as well as limbs and extremities that vary in proportion (see *Appendix A: SCP-2523-1* for additional detail). These entities carry out routine retail operations, except for attempting to persuade customers to make non-monetary exchanges. At the end of this 24-hour period they are relieved by scheduled human employees who typically begin closing the store for the season.

Exposed persons will rationalize all anomalous properties of SCP-2523, including those of trades, entities, and objects originating from the anomaly, as entirely normal experiences. This effect extends to direct conversation with affected persons as well as photographs and other direct recordings. This is an antimemetic effect that Class W mnestic treatment combined with conscious reaffirmation of observed details has been demonstrated to neutralize.

When a customer attempts to purchase an item during the anomaly, SCP-2523-1 entities will attempt to persuade them not to use monetary means to purchase the item. Instead, the entity will ask for a trade. Entities have accepted physical objects as well as more abstract concepts as fair trades. This has included: hair, personal abilities, years of life, children, illegal drugs, memories, and emotions (for a full list see *Appendix B: SCP-2523 Non-Monetary Exchange*). If the customer insists on paying with money the entity will, with visible reluctance, accept. Customers appear to have permanently lost the traded quality in all cases that it was testable.

Any item acquired by non-monetary means will manifest significant anomalous properties. The following is a partial list (see *Appendix B* for the full list):

Item	Anomalous Properties	Exchanged For
Prosthetic vampire fangs	Wearer develops an uncontrollable desire to consume blood (any vertebrate blood is accepted) as well as the ability to induce a state of extreme suggestibility via conversation.	30 grams of heroin
A dark chocolate	After consuming the bar, the subject lost all interest in food and did not	The memory of a childhood family trip

candy bar	show any signs of starvation despite consuming nothing else for 28 days.	
300 plastic spiders	Purchaser was inspired to consume the spiders. Following consumption of a spider, subject was able to excrete an otherwise non-anomalous living banded spider (*Argiope trifasciata*) from bodily orifices, and direct it telepathically	The ability to sing
"Sexy Nurse" costume	Wearer demonstrated markedly decreased sexual inhibitions as well as increased attractiveness to the opposite sex. Sexual partners reported mild anesthetic effects.	An eight year old boy, current whereabouts are unknown
Decorative trick mirror	Entities visible in mirror are deceased persons or pets known to the viewer	Empathy
Bag of Roasted Pumpkin Seeds	Seeds originate from SCP-097	A tattoo depicting the rank chevrons of a United States Navy Petty Officer 1st Class. Tattoo was removed without scarring

Addenda:

Ejection Events: The first ejection event occurred during initial containment on 11/01/1999 at 0110 hours and is typical of all later ejection events. Agent Mugnaini attempted to physically block the entrance to the anomaly. A SCP-2523-1 entity emerged and asked Agent Mugnaini to leave. Mugnaini refused, and began to suffer significant full body pain, which increased in intensity until he complied. Afterwards Mugnaini reported having "bad luck", and statistical analysis determined that he, and Area-█ where he was stationed, were suffering a significantly high number of unfortunate coincidences. This condition ended with his death in a car accident on 01/25/2000. It is suspected as a contributing factor in 17 injuries, four fatalities, and one Category-3 Breach Event at Area-█. Further testing has determined that this effect persists for 366 days. Once ejected, personnel are unable to reenter the anomaly, even after the 366-day period has expired.

Detention of SCP-2523-1 Entity:

Interviewed: SCP-2523-1 entity with nametag reading "Bobby Goodman".

Interviewer: Agent Rossetti

Foreword: On 10/31/2001 at 2000 hours MTF o-13 agents abducted an SCP-2523-1 entity to Site-17 for questioning and containment. It is described as having canine ears, a primate muzzle, and disproportionately long arms and legs (see *Appendix A* for a full description). Entity was successfully secured with iron restraints. Three o-13 team members were ejected from the anomaly as a consequence of the operation.

<Begin Log, 11/01/2001 0200 hours>

Rossetti: So, "Bobby", would you like to tell me about where you work?

SCP-2523-1: I don't work, human. I sell things.

Rossetti: Tell me about the things you sell, then.

SCP-2523-1: We sell delicious things, wonderful things, things of joy and darkness, things from the land of youth, things from the land of death, and the things from the border country. Come buy!

Rossetti: Who are you?

SCP-2523-1: [laughs] You humans! Always so forgetful! Such a delight! At summer's end, the gates at the border country are opened wide! We have come to sell our wares at this time as we did in the, what is your word for the places in the shadow that cannot be reached from the now? The past? We are the in-between people, the border people. Vassals neither to hot radiant summer, or cold merciless winter. We are the Autumn People.

Rossetti: Why only seasonal Halloween stores, and not others?

SCP-2523-1: Oh! The in-between places, they are ours. They too live only here, in the edge of summer.

Rossetti: Why do you prefer to trade for things, and not money?

SCP-2523-1: Money has no value. It is only a medium of exchange. We crave only things of value, for these we can trade in the world. How do you think we get the things we sell? We are the Autumn People, not cobblers!

Rossetti: Are you aware that the things you sell are problematic for humans?

SCP-2523-1: Yes! Of course they are! We are a merry people! Our wares are mirthful!

<End Log>

Closing Statement: Following the interview the entity was transferred to a humanoid containment unit and was extremely cooperative. At sunset on 11/01/2001 the entity vanished from containment leaving behind a crude doll made of rough unworked oak sticks, clothing scraps and mineral clay. All milk products at Site-17 were reported to have instantly spoiled simultaneously with this event.

Footnotes

1. The similarities between this phenomenon and SCP-1323, including the overlapping time frame, spatial distortion, the behavior of the entities within, and the nature of the exchanges suggest that these may be highly correlated phenomena. Questioning the SCP-2523-1 entities about this connection has resulted in ejection events.

SCP-1323

Item #: SCP-1323

Object Class: Euclid

Special Containment Procedures: Baseline containment of access points to SCP-1323 consists of passive monitoring of nearby communities in order to identify solicitations for contributions to SCP-1323's contests. Solicitations typically appear approximately 7-10 weeks prior to each access point's activation in the form of large parchment or vellum notices glued onto the sides of various buildings. Once a solicitation has been identified, D-class with relevant skills are to be selected and provided appropriate materials to create an entry for each competition. Entries are to be delivered to the access point immediately once they have been completed, and no later than 10 days prior to the activation of the access point.

Active containment is only necessary once an access point activates, and consists of erecting security checkpoints immediately outside the access point under the guise of "anti-terrorism security measures". All individuals attempting to enter SCP-1323 will be provided a "membership wristband" which is to contain a miniature GPS tracker, wireless camera, microphone and transmitter. Attempts to fully prevent civilians from entering SCP-1323 have resulted in individuals spontaneously appearing in SCP-1323, usually escorted by an employee of SCP-1323.

Description: SCP-1323 denotes both an anomalous region of space that can only be accessed from one of four access points located in the British counties of [REDACTED] and the event that occurs within this region. The interior of SCP-1323 resembles a large open field, with permanently cloudy or overcast skies. Travel in any direction will result in a return to the main activity space. Each access point is active for 7-12 consecutive days at some point during the months of October and November. Only one access point is active at any given time. Each access point is located no more than 1.5 km from the closest SCP-2952 terminal.

Located in this field is a fairground, consisting of an exhibition hall, a livestock pavilion, and a sideshow. Interspersed throughout the fairgrounds are a variety of information and ticket kiosks, food stalls, and wandering entertainers. All buildings appear to be made of heavily weathered and cracked granite blocks, and non-permanent structures such as game stalls are typically constructed of aged wood, threadbare cloth, and lightly corroded non-ferrous metals.

The exhibition hall contains a large array of entries into various judging competitions. All entries are homemade and categories have included quilts, jams and jellies, photography (with separate categories for black and white, color, and Kirlian), swords and daggers, gemstone statuary, watercolor paintings, embroidery, and musical instruments. The top three winners in each category will have a leather sack[1] appear within their primary residence coinciding with the deactivation of the applicable access point. Each sack contains 13 coins composed of a pure metal, weighing 1 pound (0.4536 kg) each, with the first place winner receiving gold coins, the second place winner receiving silver coins, and the third place winner receiving copper coins.

Entrants in any category receive "free passes" to SCP-1323 and are allowed access to "employee restricted" areas. Surveillance recorded from D-class personnel reveal that this restricted area appears to be underground, with earthen walls and ceilings. Although entrants are generally confined to large rooms, D-class have previously been able to access other areas, which appear to be a complex system of passageways whose layout is topologically inconsistent. Fairground employees can occasionally be seen moving through these passages, although they will uniformly escort non-employees back to the original chamber if seen.

The livestock pavilion is separated into quarters, each containing a different category of animal. These are bovines (various breeds of cattle), equines (various breeds of horses and unicorns), canines (various breeds of hunting dogs and wolves), and porcines (pigs, hogs and boars). In addition to the judged competitions for best example of each animal category, there are irregular exhibition demonstrations involving the animals, such as trick riding, obstacle courses, and death matches.

The sideshow consists of a variety of games, rides, and attractions. These include standard attractions such as ring-toss, bobbing for apples, skee-ball, carousels, ferris wheels and mirror mazes, as well as anomalous attractions such as shooting ranges[2], freak-shows, and "guess your weight" booths[3]. Participation in any of these requires from 1 to 15 tickets.

The food stalls sell typical fair food, such as roasted poultry legs, deep-fried sweets (ice cream, snack cakes, chocolate sandwich cookies, and ambrosia have all been previously identified), candy floss, caramel apples, beer, and lemonade. Prices range from 5-10 tickets. Approximately 17% of all patrons known to have ingested these foodstuffs fail to leave SCP-1323 before the local access point deactivates, and have been later identified as fair employees.

The information kiosks provide maps of the fairgrounds, program schedules, and sell the tickets that are used throughout the fair. Ticket prices are constant across appearances of SCP-1323 and consist of the following:

1 ticket	a joyful laugh and a sorrowful tear
5 tickets	a cherished memory
10 tickets	a year and a day
25 tickets	a lost love
100 tickets	a favor

Civilians and Foundation personnel who purchase tickets will display a variety of mental, emotional, and behavioral abnormalities for up to 7 years, and frequently report a compulsion or sense of foreboding if they are prevented from following any unusual or abnormal impulses during that time.

Fairground employees are all dressed in clothing and costumes consistent with styles from the early 20th century. The behavior and terminology of the employees is strongly reminiscent of stereotypical carnival barkers from that same time period. Only 37% of employees appear to be human, while the remainder are anomalous humanoids. Their morphology varies considerably from individual to individual, including heights ranging from approximately 75-215 cm; skin tones including pure white, various shades of blue and green, and dark brown; and exaggerated or non-standard placement of facial features. All attempts to interview employees, or interact with them in any way other than as part of their duties, are rebuffed with suggestions to "take it up with management." No member of "management" has ever been located despite repeated requests for interviews and exploration of restricted areas.

Any aggressive actions taken towards the employees, other patrons, fairground structures, or contest entries result in the rapid appearance[4] of large, muscular entities who eject the offending individual from the active access point. Individuals so ejected are unable to enter any access point in the future, and typically display minor cosmetic changes such as unnatural skin pigmentation changes, rapid cartilage growth of the face and head, and increased body hair growth rate. These cosmetic changes are permanent, and will rapidly restore themselves if surgically corrected.

Due to the overlapping time frames that SCP-1323 and SCP-2523 can be accessed, as well as the demeanors of the respective proprietors, a connection has been hypothesized. Inquiries regarding SCP-2523 have resulted in the aforementioned large entities appearing and demanding a cessation of this line of questioning. Failure to comply has resulted in permanent ejection, similar to threatening fairground staff.

Footnotes

1. DNA analysis of the leather matches *Bos taurus*.

2. The targets are small live humanoids, labelled as "goblins" or "pixies" by the game stall employees.

3. All D-class who have tried this type of game have had their weights immediately and radically altered to match that guessed, regardless of the degree of the mass change.

4. Longest recorded response time was 2.6 seconds

GLOSSARY

Article Format

Listed by typical order of appearance in an SCP article.

- **Item #** — The numeric identifier for the SCP. Note that the formal name of an SCP is always "SCP-####", and not its number alone ("SCP-173", not "173"), although the number on its own is often used informally.

- **Object Class** — A system of categorization based roughly on the difficulty of containing the entity or object. See the Object Classes guide for more information, and definitions of the most commonly used object classes (**Safe, Euclid, Keter**), as well as some less commonly used object classes (including **Thaumiel, Neutralized** and **Apollyon**). Alternative classification systems or more esoteric object classes may sometimes be used.

- **Special Containment Procedures** (SCP) — Instructions to be followed to keep the entity or object contained. May be referred to informally as "conprocs".

- **Description** — The section of an SCP article that explains in a clear and concise way what the entity or object does, and why it is contained. The description can be supplemented by one or more addenda, but you should be able to understand the basic function through the Description alone.

- **Addendum** — (*Plural: addenda*) A section of an SCP article that either expands on specific aspects of the primary Description, shows the progression of information over time, or otherwise provides additional insight that does not fit into the Description block. Addenda can be posted on the main page or in separate **supplement** pages, and can include Experiment Logs, Exploration Logs, Incident Reports or Interviews.

Foundation Terminology

Other terms used in Foundation documents to describe their own personnel, facilities and containment procedures.

- **The Administrator** — Mysterious figure in-universe, may (or may not) have been the Founder of the SCP Foundation. Possibly a member of the **O5 Council**, possibly the overall leader of the Foundation.

- **agent** — An undercover Foundation field agent, typically capitalized when used as a title (e.g. Agent Smith). Note that not all field personnel employed by the Foundation are necessarily "agents" in this sense, nor do all such personnel have the title "Agent". See also: **containment team, response team, Mobile Task Force,** and **researcher.**

- **Anomalous Item** — An object with **anomalous** properties too minor to warrant **Special Containment Procedures** or further research.

- **anomaly/anomalous** — Foundation term for the objects they contain and research. Generally defined as anything that cannot be explained by current scientific knowledge.

- **Area** — A type of Foundation Facility completely unknown to the public.

- **containment breach** — Term used when an SCP object escapes containment. Could involve physically breaking out of a **containment chamber**, could also mean spread of knowledge about it outside of the Foundation.

- **containment chamber** — A room dedicated to the containment of an SCP object.

- **containment team** — Field personnel specializing in recovering or retrieving anomalous objects or entities. Members may or may not be field agents as well, but usually have a different title, such as "Containment Specialist". See also **agent, response team.**

- **[DATA EXPUNGED]** — One of the two types of censorship used on the site, something that is "expunged" has been permanently deleted from all records, typically because the information poses a hazard in and of itself, e.g. if it's a **memetic** hazard. See also **[REDACTED].**

- **D Class** — Foundation employees deemed expendable if necessary for testing or containment. See the Security Clearance Levels guide for more information.

- **Decommissioned (D)** — An anomalous object that has been intentionally destroyed. See the Object Classes guide for more information.

- **department** — Organizations within the Foundation that specialize in a specific task, discipline or field.

- **director** — The head of a Foundation **Facility** or **Department**. Typically capitalized when used as a title (e.g. Director Jones).

- **Explained (EX)** — A sub-class of SCP object that has either been debunked as a hoax, sufficiently understood so as to be normal scientific knowledge, or so widely disseminated that containment is no longer possible.

- **Extranormal Events** — Anomalous events that occurred too briefly to be contained.

- **Facility** — A generic term used to refer to both **Sites** and **Areas**.

- **The Foundation** — A secret organization that contains anomalous or supernatural objects, entities, and phenomena through the creation of Special Containment Procedures. Usually just "The Foundation", only rarely referred to as the "SCP Foundation" in-universe.

- **Groups of Interest (GoI)** — Organizations other than the Foundation that are aware of the anomalous.

- **K-Class Scenario** — Hypothetical situations with drastic effects on normality or reality. The most well-known K-Class Event, the XK-Class Event, typically denotes a catastrophic event resulting in the destruction of human society, if not the entire human species.

- **Location of Interest** (LoI) — A location with known or suspected anomalous properties. See also **Unexplained Location, Nexus** and **Freeport.**

- **Mobile Task Force** — A Mobile Task Force (or MTF for short) is a highly-trained and specialized team that is deployed to various locations as needed to deal with specialized threats or conditions. Mobile Task Forces are designated by a Greek letter and a number (e.g. "MTF Alpha-7", "MTF Omega-15") and may have a nickname attached, similar to many real-life military units. MTFs are the elite personnel of the Foundation, and run the gamut from highly experienced field researchers to combat-hardened troops.

- **Normalcy/Normality/Baseline Reality/Consensus Reality** — The apparently ordinary state of the world, which the Foundation preserves by containing anomalies. See also **The Veil.**

- **O5 Council** (O5) — short for the "Council of Observers, Level 5" or the "Overseer Level 5 Council". The highest authority in the Foundation, a council of 12 or 13 individuals who have the power to authorize or veto any action taken by the Foundation as a whole. O5 Council members are only known by their numbers (O5-1 through O5-13), are rarely involved in day-to-day Foundation activities, and are typically not allowed to contact any SCP objects directly for fear of contamination. Note that it's a capital letter "o", not the number zero.

- **Person of Interest** (PoI) — Individuals that the **Foundation** is investigating or observing due to their involvement with the anomalous. May have anomalous abilities, have had contact with an **SCP object** or be a member of a **Group of Interest.**

- **[REDACTED]** — One of the two types of censorship used on the site. Something that is "redacted" is withheld from the article because the reader is not cleared to see the information, but would be made available to someone else with a higher **Security Clearance Level** or on a need-to-know basis. See also **[DATA EXPUNGED].**

- **researcher** — A broad term for anyone involved in research and development at the Foundation - they may be referred to as a Researcher, Technician, Doctor or Professor, depending on their qualifications and specialty. Researchers can be involved in anything from figuring out how an anomalous object or entity functions to developing better materials and containment procedures. Field researchers may also accompany containment teams to assess the nature of uncontained anomalies.

- **response team** — A heavily armed team trained to deal with security or containment breaches, typically at a secure Foundation site. Response team members are also sent into the field to escort containment teams when dealing with highly hostile or dangerous objects or entities, or when enemy Groups of Interest are involved.

- **Security Clearance Level** — Specifies the information that a Foundation employee is authorized to know, ranging from 1 (very limited) to 5 (beyond top secret).

- **SCP** — An initialism for "Special Containment Procedures", and used informally as a short-form of "SCP article", as in, "I wrote three SCPs yesterday". SCP objects or entities should not be formally referred to as "an SCP" or "the SCP" in-universe, although characters might do so informally, even using casual pronunciations like "scip" or "skip". Note that "SCP" is *not* an initialism for "Secure, Contain, Protect"; the motto of the Foundation is a backronym derived from "SCP".

- **SCP object/SCP entity** — An anomaly assigned its own **Special Containment Procedures**.

- **Site** — A type of Foundation Facility disguised behind a mundane front (e.g. as a corporation or government office).

- **Species of Interest** (**SoI**) — Non-human species with anomalous properties.

- **Undesignated Anomaly (UA)** — An anomalous entity that has not yet been placed into containment. Temporary designation, prior to full documentation as an SCP object.

- **Unexplained Location** — A specific place where anomalous phenomena too minor to be assigned **Special Containment Procedures** occur. See also **Location of Interest**, as well as **Nexus** and **Freeport** for inhabited anomalous locations.

- **The Veil** — A term referring to the separation of the anomalous and the people aware of it from the ordinary world. Actively maintained by organizations like the Foundation that conceal anomalies.

Anomalous Science

Terms used by the Foundation and by other groups to describe and categorize the anomalous.

- **Acroamatic Abatement** — The processing of waste products and esoteric substance from anomalies into non-anomalous industrial effluent. See Everything You Need to Know About Acroamatic Abatement But Were Too Confused by the Name to Ask for an elaboration.

- **Akiva Radiation** — Radiation linked to prayer and divine intervention, possible to measure and quantify in centiAkiva. A place with high levels of Akiva radiation has been visited or touched by a god, while a place with low Akiva radiation may be considered forgotten or forsaken by the gods. Named after a Jewish scholar and religious leader, the Rabbi Akiva.

- **Anart** — Short for Anomalous Art. This can be artwork with anomalous properties, or the use of the anomalous for the purpose of artistic expression. See this document and this lecture for further analysis.

- **Anartists** — Short for Anomalous Artists, and refers to anyone capable of creating **Anart**, such as members of Are We Cool Yet? or the Medicean Academy of Occult Art.

- **antimemetic** — Antimemes (also known as Counter concepts) are ideas which, by their intrinsic nature, discourage or prevent people from spreading them. The Foundation has an Antimemetics Division investigating and containing anomalous antimemes.

- **Apex Tier Pluripotent Entity** — An incredibly powerful being, possibly omnipotent. Generally used as a clinical term for a god.

- **Aspect Radiation** — **EVE** emissions intense enough to alter reality - the basis of **thaumatology**.

- **bozomorphic** — Clinical term for entities resembling clowns.

- **bureaucratohazards** — A sub-class of **semiohazards** that affect bureaucratic systems, making certain entities not guilty despite committing crimes or violating rules.

- **carnomancy/fleshcrafting** — anomalous techniques for altering and reshaping the body, most frequently practiced by adherents of Sarkicism.

- **Cognitive Resistance Value** — A measurement of the mental fortitude and resistance of an individual to mind-affecting anomalous effects, particularly those that are **memetic**.

- **cognitohazard** — A term used to refer to objects that are dangerous to perceive. This could occur through any or all of the human senses, including sight, sound, smell, taste, or touch. Differs from an **infohazard** in that simply being informed about the **cognitohazard** has no anomalous effect. See also **memetics**.

- **ectoentropic** — Entities or objects that violate the first and/or second law of thermodynamics, generating matter or energy in a way that decreases entropy (the natural increase in disorder and randomness over time). Applies to any anomaly that produces energy or matter in an unexplained way.

- **Elan-Vital Energy (EVE)** — Mysterious energy emitted from living beings and sapient anomalies that can power **thaumatology**. See this lecture for more information.

- **essophysics** — The scientific study of the physical embodiments or manifestations of abstract concepts.

- **Freeport** — A larger and more formally recognised type of **Nexus**, an area that is inherently anomalous and entirely behind the **Veil**. This means that there is no need to try to conceal the existence of the **anomalous** from the people who live there, since they all already know.

- **Hemovore** — A clinical term for a vampire.

- **Hume** — A unit used to measure the strength or amount of reality in an area. See the FAQ for more information. Named for the philosopher David Hume.

- **infoallergenic** — An uncommon class of infohazard, capable of exhibiting both **memetic** and **antimemetic** properties.

- **infohazard** — A term used to refer to objects that have an anomalous effect whenever they are referred to or described. Differs from a **cognitohazard** in that cognitohazards require the anomalous phenomenon to be directly perceived, whereas infohazards may be spread indirectly, simply through people telling each other about them. Because of this, the effects of **infohazards** are often **memetic**. See this orientation for more information.

- **Kinetohazard/Kinetoglyphs** — anomalous mental and physical effects that occur when an entity performs specific gestures and movements.

- **Large-Scale Aggressor (LSA)** — Clinical term for a giant monster.

- **memetic** — Memes are ideas or behaviors that can be transmitted to others through communication or imitation, and are the basic units of culture. In the context of the Foundation, memetic effects are a sub-class of **cognitohazards** and **infohazards** that deal with transfer of information. Ideas and concepts with anomalous memetic properties can spread much more effectively than non-anomalous memes, and may have anomalous effects on anyone exposed to them. Creators and users of memetic hazards are referred to as memeticists. See Understanding Memetics and this orientation for more information.

- **metamorph/polymorph** — Clinical term for shapeshifters; entities that can change their form and/or shape.

- **narremes** — The basic units of a narrative, much like **memes** are the basic units of a culture.

- **narrativohazard** — A construct of independent, individual units of narratives (known as **narremes**) that collectively destroys relevant stories.

- **Nexus** — An actively anomalous location supporting a permanent community.

- **noogenesis** — Clinical term for the formation of a new consciousness.

- **Noosphere** — The realm of human thought, encompassing dreams, concepts and ideas.

- **ontokinesis/ontokinetic** — Clinical term for **Reality Bending**.

- **pataphysics/'pataphysics** — The scientific study of fictional narratives, including the fictional SCP universe itself.

- **Pattern Screamer** — Consciousnesses located in the very fabric of reality, defying the laws of reality and existence.

122

- **pretermemetic** — Information that is selectively **memetic** or **anti-memetic** depending on the nature of the recipients or circumstances. Used by groups such as Herman Fuller's Circus of the Disquieting to advertise without attracting the attention of organizations like the **Foundation**.

- **Reality Bending/Reality Warping** — The anomalous ability to alter reality. May be referred to as **ontokinesis** or magic, although **thaumatology** is generally regarded as something separate. Humanoid Reality Benders may be referred to as "Type Greens" using Global Occult Coalition terminology, or as "Ontokineticists". See this FAQ and this orientation for more information.

- **Semiontological anomaly/semiohazard** — Anomalies that disrupt the **Semiosphere** (the medium through which information about reality travels before it is perceived or measured) to create universal axioms that should not be possible.

- **Spectral Entity** — Clinical term for a ghost or spirit. May also be referred to as an ectomorph, an entity made from ectoplasm.

- **Spectremetry** — The scientific study of **Spectral Entities.**

- **surrealistics** — The scientific study of anomalies too incomprehensible or bizarre to understand, except through illogical thought and the use of **agnostics.**

- **Tartarean Resonance Energy** (**TRE**) — Radiation naturally produced by demonic entities. Named for Tartarus, the part of the Greek Underworld where monsters and sinners are imprisoned.

- **Thaumatology** — The scientific study of magic, known as **thaumaturgy** (a term meaning "wonder-working" and referring to magic or miracles). Users of Magic can be referred to as Thaumatologists, Thaumaturges or "Type Blues" in Global Occult Coalition terminology. When considered to be distinct from **Reality Bending**, the phenomena studied by thaumatology generally follow more predictable rules and limitations. See this lecture and this orientation for more information.

- **tychekinesis** — Clinical term for probability manipulation, named for the Greek goddess of fate and fortune, Tyche.

- **Way** — A anomalous connection between two locations, enabling rapid travel between them regardless of distance. Ways can facilitate travel into other universes, including to the Wanderer's Library. See this orientation for more information.

Anomalous Technologies

Advanced technologies existing within the Foundation setting.

- **agnostics** — Substances that makes consumers more open to otherwise incomprehensible anomalous phenomena by altering their thought-patterns to become more illogical. See also **surrealistics.**

- **amnestic** — Drugs, procedures, or devices that induce memory loss when administered to an individual. While there are real chemicals with amnestic properties, the Foundation's amnestics have much greater potency and specificity, enabling them to make civilian witnesses forget about anomalous activity. Although the exact details vary, see the Amnestic Use Guide and the Updated Amnestics Guide for more information.

- **Apportation** — Teleportation through **thaumaturgy**.

- **Artificially Intelligent Conscript (AIC)** — An artificial intelligence created and employed by the Foundation's Artificial Intelligence Applications Division.

- **beryllium bronze** — A metallic alloy frequently used in anomalous devices.

- **counter-meme** — A **memetic** concept, protecting against or reversing the effects of an anomalous meme.

- **Deepwell server** — Specialized data storage servers capable of preserving information across shifts in reality. See SCP-4800 for more information.

- **demonics** — A type of **paratechnology** that incorporates sentient entities referred to as "demons". See this history for more information.

- **eigenweapon** — An anomalous weapon of mass destruction. See this tale for one history of eigenweapon development. Terms like eigenmachine may be used for similar devices intended for purposes other than destruction.

- **Geas** — The use of memetic agents to force a person to obey a set of rules or guidelines. The name comes from Irish mythology, where a Geas is a magically enforced prohibition against certain actions.

- **Gnostics** — The opposite of an **agnostic**, Gnostics make one more certain and surer of things, although this does not necessarily make them correct.

- **Kant Counter** - Instrument used to measure the **Hume** level of a location, that is, the amount of reality. See this FAQ for more information. Named for the philosopher Immanuel Kant.

- **Memetic Kill Agent** — A **memetic** hazard with a lethal effect on anyone exposed to it without the appropriate inoculation with a **counter-meme**. Used to protect SCP-001 and other important data from unauthorized access.

- **mnestic** — The opposite of an **amnestic**, mnestics are chemical compounds that enhance the user's memory. This can be used to bring back erased or forgotten memories, counter the effects of amnestics, and resist **antimemetic** effects. See the Antimemetics Division Series and the Updated Amnestics Guide for more information.

- **Paratechnology (Paratech)** — Technology that relies on anomalous principles or components to function. More specific terms like paraweapon and parapharmaceutical may be used for specific types of paratechnology.

- **Scranton Reality Anchor** — A technology that stabilizes reality around it, preventing or restricting **Reality Bending.** Occasionally called a Scranton Box, although that may refer to a somewhat different technology. See this FAQ and this Grant Request for more information, and this page for blueprints. May have been named after the in-universe inventor, one "Robert Scranton".

- **Telekill** (SCP-148) — A metal with the property of blocking or preventing anomalous extrasensory mental effects like telepathy and mind control.

- **Xyank-Anastasakos Constant Temporal Sink/Xyank-Anastasakos Constant Time Sink** — Named after Dr. Thaddeus Xyank and Dr. Athena Anastasakos of the Foundation's Department of Temporal Anomalies. Capable of protecting a place or an object from temporal changes, or altering the passage of time to speed it up or slow it down within a specific area.

CREDITS

SCP-3121 - Get Out of My Head by Buttfranklin

SCP-082 - "Fernand" the Cannibal by FritzWillie

SCP-140 - An Incomplete Chronicle by AssertiveRoland

SCP-1726 - The Library and the Pillar by Djoric

SCP-2615 - If You Believe by KnightKnight

SCP-2547 - Dog Days Of Summer by AbsentmindedNihilist

SCP-2303 - Tower of Silence by Kalinin

SCP-4028 - La Historia de Don Quixote de la Mancha by TheGreatHippo

SCP-3353 - Secrets for Sweets by Zyn

SCP-1918 - Tik Tak Tow by Faminepulse

SCP-1000 - Bigfoot by thedeadlymoose

SCP-3844 - To Slay A Dragon by CaptainKirby

SCP-435 - "He-Who-Made-Dark" by sandrewswann

SCP-2264 - In the Court of Alagadda by MetaPhysician

SCP-2523 - Goblin Market by sirpudding

SCP-1323 by Drewbear

SCP FOUNDATION: https://scp-wiki.wikidot.com/

Made in the USA
Las Vegas, NV
19 November 2022